"If you ever need me, I'm right down the street. Well, you know that."

Hudson stuffed his hands into the pockets of his jeans. He considered Clair's expression. *Does she wonder who I was with at the River Grill? Maybe I should tell her straight out—that the woman won a lunch with me in a charity auction. And what's the deal with Glenn Yves? Is Clair dating him?* He had no idea how to bring up a topic as prickly as cacti, but maybe he could just hover over the subject. "I was surprised to see you at the River Grill today. I've never seen you there before."

"I've never been there before."

"Well, that must be why. . .I've never seen you there before." *I'm just going in circles here. Maybe I'd better just cut to the chase.* "I'm playing at the Silver Moon Café tomorrow evening. It's a restaurant, and they have performers who. . .perform." *Oh brother.* "Would you like to go with me?"

"Yes." Clair's hand flew up to her mouth. "Yes, I would. Yes."

"All righty then." Hudson smiled, feeling confident she really wanted to go with him. Suddenly he was in the mood for his coffee again. Lots of coffee. He reached for his beverage as his enthusiasm radiated through his fingers, causing a squeezing action on his grip. He couldn't stop the gush as he watched the coffee make a slow-motion kind of rise and fall all over his very favorite shirt.

ANITA HIGMAN hopes to give her audience a "gasp and a giggle" when they read her stories. She's the award-winning author of eighteen books. Anita has a B.A. in speech communication and is a member of American Christian Fiction Writers. Anita enjoys hiking with her family, visiting show caves, and cooking brunch for her friends. Please drop by her book café for a cyber visit at www.anitahigman.com.

Books by Anita Higman

HEARTSONG PRESENTS
HP734—Larkspur Dreams—coauthored with Janice A. Thompson

JANICE A. THOMPSON is a Christian author from Texas. She has four grown daughters, and the whole family is active in ministry, particularly the arts. Janice is a writer by trade, but wears many other hats, as well. She previously taught drama and creative writing at a Christian school of the arts. She also directed a global drama missions team. She currently heads up the elementary department at her church and enjoys public speaking. Janice is passionate about her faith and does all she can to share it with others, which is why she particularly loves writing inspirational novels. Through her stories, she hopes to lead others into a relationship with a loving God.

Books by Janice A. Thompson

HEARTSONG PRESENTS
HP490—A Class of Her Own
HP593—Angel Incognito
HP613—A Chorus of One
HP666—Sweet Charity
HP667—Banking On Love
HP734—Larkspur Dreams—coauthored with Anita Higman
HP754—Red Like Crimson

The Love Song

Anita Higman and Janice A. Thompson

Heartsong Presents

To Irene Powers (Aunt Reny Beanie), your joy and whimsical outlook has sweetened every life it's touched, especially mine.

Much gratitude goes to Pat Durham for her help in understanding the life of an image coach. Appreciation goes to Chris Colter for answering my questions about paramedics. And a big thank you goes to Robin Miller, Joanne Brokaw, and my daughter, Hillary, for their enthusiastic help.

Anita Higman

To my Lord and Savior, Jesus Christ—my Shepherd. I can hear You singing Your "love song" over me, even now.

Janice A. Thompson

A note from the Author:
We love to hear from our readers! You may correspond with us by writing:

Anita Higman and Janice A. Thompson
Author Relations
PO Box 721
Uhrichsville, OH 44683

ISBN 978-1-59789-886-7

THE LOVE SONG

Our mission is to publish and distribute inspirational products offering exceptional value and biblical encouragement to the masses.

PRINTED IN THE U.S.A.

one

I don't belong here. Clair stared at the crowd inside the banquet room as she clutched her dress like a lost child.

Just beyond the gilded doors, laughter rose up through the party like soda bubbles. She wondered what clever remark had been said to amuse the guests, but unless she ventured inside, she would never know. *Three steps. That's all it takes.*

Clair stared down at her simple evening gown with a sigh. A dreary and familiar pain washed over her. Even if she dared enter, she would be invisible. But then maybe going unseen was easiest after all.

Perhaps she shouldn't have agreed to come. Oh, how she wished Ima had been feeling better. Ima liked parties. Clair didn't want to disappoint her employer, but she didn't know how to face such a large gathering of what she called "the beautifuls." Maybe she could just slip out of the River Walk Hotel and make her apologies to Ima in the morning. She took in a deep breath and, with regret, turned to leave.

A man, one of "the beautifuls," emerged from the music and laughter. He breezed by her, and then spun back around. "Are you leaving? The party is just getting started."

Clair glanced up at him, startled, then stared down at her shoes. "Are you talking. . .to me?"

"Well, I'm certain you're the only one sharing the foyer with me," he said.

She ventured a look up at the stranger. The man appeared to be in his midthirties, and his hazel eyes flashed with gold, reminding her of the brooch Ima had given her for Christmas. In fact, he shined so handsomely before her, she thought he must be a phantom. He winked. Clair could feel the flush of heat rising in her face at the sudden attention.

"Did you just arrive?" he asked with perfect diction.

Clair only nodded, and then scolded herself for not speaking.

"Then why would you want to leave? If you don't mind my asking."

"I. . .don't belong here." She admonished herself for being so bold with a stranger.

He strolled toward her. "Anyone invited here tonight *belongs* here. Come on now, you don't want to leave without meeting the author. Leslie Mandel has an uncanny sense of humor." He smoothed his tie. "And the guests are having a wonderful time. I think you will enjoy yourself, too, if you give it a chance. Please say you'll stay."

The stranger's words, as well as the soothing music, began to woo her. Her resistance faded. "Who are you?" she asked in a whisper. *Oh no.* Had she breeched another societal convention of some kind? Too quiet, and then too blunt? Her unfamiliarity with social graces always seemed to be her undoing, which was one of the many reasons she enjoyed spending most of her days tucked away in Ima's Bookshop, like a forgotten volume of a book no one cared to read. It was easy. Quiet. Certainly less stressful than mainstream life.

The handsome gentleman laughed in a rich bass voice. "Who am I? Good philosophical question. I've been asking myself that for years and have only recently found my answer inside the pages of the greatest book of all time." He placed his palms together. "Where are my manners? Sorry, I didn't introduce myself. I'm Glenn Yves, image coach." He bowed slightly.

"I'm Clair. . .O'Neal." *Am I supposed to reach out my hand first?* In introductions, her hands sometimes flailed around like the tail on a kite. Not knowing for sure about proper etiquette, she decided to twiddle her fingers behind her back.

"So glad to meet you, Ms. O'Neal," he said. "I'd love to introduce you to the author. This party launches her latest book, but she's also one of my former clients. Leslie Mandel is one of Little Rock's finest."

Clair thought of an excuse to get away, but she could only manage to stutter unintelligibly.

Glenn held out his arm to her as if she were his date. "May I escort you inside?"

Too late to run. She remembered her promise to Ima to represent the bookshop at the party. She would do it for Ima. Somehow. She whispered a prayer for help.

Glenn looked into her eyes, waiting for her response.

Clair finally accepted his arm. Glenn then whisked her into the magical land of "the beautifuls." As they walked, she ventured a glance up at his face. He stood tall, with shoulders straight, head held high. She took in the aroma of his cologne. No doubt expensive, because of the way it made her head go giddy.

Clair tried not to gape at all the pretty decorations. Thousands of twinkling lights illuminated the room like winking fairies. Three guitar players sat strumming classical music on a small stage. Not far away sat a huge ice sculpture in the center of a buffet table.

A couple of the guests offered up polite nods as she and Glenn walked through the crowd. In spite of this, Clair felt a little unnerved. Were they looking at her dress? She knew her secondhand gown didn't measure up to the others in the room, but it was the nicest thing she owned, and the soft brown color went with her hair. *Didn't it?* She glanced at herself in a wall mirror. Her shoulders slumped even more as she looked at herself. *Too thin, too pale, too awkward. I look as feminine as a cigar. Why does this man even want to talk to me?*

Glenn looked down at her and treated her to another stunning smile.

Clair felt dizzy, as though she were riding on an out-of-control merry-go-round. Her heart skipped a beat as she broke out in perspiration. She reached out to a nearby table to steady herself.

"You're trembling. Don't be afraid of these people. I'm sure they have fears, too. They've just learned to hide them better," Glenn whispered, and then he grinned. "The gentleman over there in the cowboy hat is Edsel Armstrong, Leslie's publicist, and the woman talking to him is Larkspur Wendell Holden. She's an artist from Eureka Springs and newly married. She'll have a show in the summer at one of the galleries here."

Clair sighed inside, trying to keep up. "I think—"

"First, let me introduce you to Leslie." Glenn swept Clair into the presence of a tall, elegant woman adorned in a brocade dress of steel blue. The author stood self-assured and theatrical looking next to a glitzy book cover, which sat on a large easel.

"Leslie"—Glenn kissed the author's flushed cheek—"I have someone I'd like you to meet. This is the beautiful Clair O'Neal. Clair, this is the illustrious Leslie Mandel."

Clair looked back and forth at them, not knowing how to reply. His choice of the word *beautiful* floored her. The irony stared her in the face. Why would he say such a thing?

"I love your name." Leslie's hand made a flourishing wave. "It sounds like an Irish actress in one of my novels. Guileless, yet. . .perceptive somehow."

While Glenn and Leslie cooed softly together like two

pigeons, Clair suddenly felt as exposed and as foolish looking as a plucked chicken. She knew what Leslie's words meant, but she wasn't sure what to say. Clair rubbed her wrist against the back of her dress, and then bunched up a ball of the material in her sweaty palm. *Silly me.* She wished she could simply crawl away unnoticed like a worm back into the earth. It would be far less torturous than the current hyperventilating folly. "Your novel," Clair finally managed, "*The Saffron Veil.* . ."

"Yes?" Leslie leaned in toward Clair with renewed interest, tapping her ruby-painted nails against her mandarin collar.

"It's selling well at our bookshop," Clair said.

Leslie bobbed her head like a puppy waiting for more treats. "Please, tell me more."

"Your novel. . ." Clair swallowed hard. "It's. . .allegorical. . . tracing the prideful journey and the descent of civilizations that chose to follow false gods." She breathed deeply to gain control of her fear.

Glenn and Leslie stared at her for a moment.

What had come out of her mouth? *It must have been garbled*, Clair thought in growing panic.

"Well." Leslie gave Clair a slow, assessing nod. "I'm impressed. Some of my biggest fans failed to make that connection."

Clair sighed. She needn't die of humiliation just yet.

Glenn's fingers brushed Leslie's hand. "Clair, did you know that Leslie's *Dream Born* has just made the *New York Times* Best Seller list?"

"Yes, and I'm so happy for you." Clair nodded in Leslie's direction, then continued to watch as both Leslie and Glenn exchanged an occasional light touch or expressive glance. No man had ever behaved in such a comfortable manner around Clair. She wondered how it would feel to be pretty and charming. Surely such a man could make her feel that way. Embarrassed, Clair forced herself back to reality and tried to pay attention.

"Actually, that's another reason my publicist put this little festivity together," Leslie said. "Promotion. . .*and* celebration. By the way, which bookstore do you work at, Clair?"

"Ima's Bookshop. It's—"

"Oh yes. I know the one. It's in the River Market District just down the street from my brother's guitar shop. I did a book signing there in my early days. I remember Ima well."

"She's grown rather frail lately. I'm—"

"Sorry to hear it." Leslie glanced over at a small cluster of people who were chuckling. "Tell her I said hello."

"If you ladies will excuse me." Glenn touched Leslie's arm. "I see someone I need to share some hearsay with." He leaned over to Clair and whispered, "Will you be all right? I'll be back in a few minutes."

Clair nodded so quickly, she felt like her head might jar itself off her neck.

Glenn smiled at her and walked over to a small swarm of "the beautifuls." She could hear him speaking to someone in what sounded like French.

Clair realized she was alone with Leslie, and she had no more ideas for chitchat. Alarm rose in her chest, making a tight circle around her heart. *Why is Leslie staring at me? What should I say?*

Several people closed in on Leslie, so Clair backed away like a turtle into its shell. She glanced around in hopes of an escape. The main doors were too far away now for comfort. She felt her throat constricting as a parched sensation seized her.

Clair spotted a silver punch bowl across the room. Surely she could risk walking across a wide, open space for a cool drink. She took a few steps forward. No one seemed to notice her activities now that she'd moved outside of Glenn's circle.

All at once the music stopped. A man tapped his glass in front of the microphone, trying to get everyone's attention.

Maybe she could just finish her journey across the room while all eyes were on the emcee. Clair stepped out again with a hesitant stride, but midway across the marble floor, something slippery made contact with her shoes. *Water?*

The world became unstable as Clair's feet slid out from underneath her. Her hands grabbed the air, and she landed with an inelegant *thump* on her backside in the middle of the room. The bottom half of her dress twisted around her legs as her evening bag slid away. Just when she'd taken in the horror of the moment, a spotlight clicked on overhead, bathing her in a shaft of light.

Quiet laughter trickled through the room.

Clair certainly didn't feel invisible now. She struggled to get to her feet, but the heel of her shoe caught on the hem of her dress. The small awakening of hope she'd felt earlier now fluttered away like an injured bird.

No tears, Clair. No tears.

two

To Clair's relief, the glaring spotlight swiveled to Leslie. The burst of applause and the refocused attention gave her a reprieve from her shame.

She looked up to discover a man with kindness in his eyes. He gently released the offending hem from her shoe and, with one sweep, lifted her off the floor.

Clair appreciated his gallantry, but knowing he'd seen her pitiful state made her shy away. In spite of her timidity, she noticed the stranger wore an endearing smile.

"That was quite a fall. Are you okay?" The stranger's breath felt warm and was scented with cinnamon.

Clair wanted to rub her sore posterior, but she didn't. "I'll be all right."

The stranger glanced down at the floor and crouched and swiped up the spill of water with some napkins. He caught the attention of one of the waiters, frowned at him, and then tossed the balled-up napkins over to him.

"Thank you," Clair said. On closer inspection, she noticed her rescuer was an athletic sort of man in his early thirties. His brown hair appeared sun lightened, and he had a faint, but noticeable, five o'clock shadow. She glanced down at his feet, trying not to stare. He wore tennis shoes with his trousers. She recalled what Ima always said about humans coming in all sorts of astonishing designs. It appeared to be true.

"By the way. . ." The stranger's face went blank. "I'm. . .I'm

Hudson Mandel. I sort of forgot who I was for a second." He laughed.

"Clair. . .O'Neal." *Does he have the same last name as the author?* Ima had mentioned Leslie Mandel was single, so perhaps he was her brother.

"Glad to meet you."

Without taking time to fret about it, Clair reached out her hand to him. The warmth and security of his touch made her want to hold on. But as she released his hand, she could tell he'd been the one to linger a bit longer. "I don't usually go to. . . parties."

He tugged on his collar as if it were a noose. "I know the feeling." He lowered his voice. "They're impossible to navigate sometimes. It's easier to be up on stage than to do this mingling thing." He grinned. "A pack of wild boars might be less grueling."

Clair felt something unfamiliar rising out of her—laughter. Something she'd forgotten how to do. She covered her mouth. The moment would hold enough joy for her to live on for a long time.

"You have a nice laugh. . .musical." Hudson had a hint of a smile. "You could put lyrics to it."

Did he actually mean such admiring praise or was he just being gregarious? "Thank you." Clair noticed Hudson appeared to be the same age as Glenn, and just as handsome, yet he seemed different—less intimidating.

Hudson pulled a package of gum out of his pocket and extended it in her direction. "Would you like a piece? Helps you to deal with the crowds. . .you know, to exchange profound and witty remarks that mean absolutely nothing. I'm sure you. . .well. . .uh. . ." He chuckled as his face flushed. "I guess I need some." He took a piece and popped it into his mouth with a smile.

"I think you're doing fine." Clair removed a stick of gum from the packet, thinking how much calmer she felt standing next to Hudson. She noticed he was the same height as she was—not tall and not short, but somewhere in between. His eyes were far from average, though—luminous, coffee colored, and memorable. "Thank you for the gum."

Hudson pressed his lips together. Then he folded his arms and looked at the floor.

His obvious uneasiness warmed Clair all over. She felt an immediate kinship with him and delighted in every second, since she knew the perfect moment would end soon.

"By the way"—Hudson gestured toward the small stage—"those are my students up there."

She glanced over at them, amazed. "You teach guitar?"

"Well, I own the River Front Guitar Shop, and I have the honor of volunteer tutoring some disadvantaged, but very dedicated, teens."

I know that shop. Clair realized Hudson was indeed Leslie's brother, since she'd mentioned his guitar shop was down the street from Ima's Bookshop. In fact, Clair had walked by his storefront countless times. She doubted anything would come of their acquaintance but still tucked the knowledge of it away in her heart. "Your students are very good." Her shoulders relaxed.

"Yes, they are. I'm proud of them."

"Classical." Clair shook her head, relishing the delicate and moving strains. "So beautiful."

"Oh yes." He looked back at her. "Beautiful," he repeated in a whisper.

How he loves his students. Clair admired his dedication.

"Do you play?" Hudson asked.

"No, not at all. But I would love to. Vocal music has always been an important part of my life, but playing an instrument has eluded me—at least so far." She surprised herself, answering so quickly and candidly. Though she loved to sing, she'd never spent much time thinking about playing the guitar until this very moment. The idea settled in, and a wave of contentment washed over her.

"Come by the shop, then. I would love to teach you."

Clair couldn't think of anything more delightful; she only wished she had the money for such a wonderful endeavor. "To be able to share your gift of music—nothing could be finer." Why was it so easy to talk to him?

"I couldn't agree more." Hudson wore a dreamy sort of expression as he hummed a tune.

The melody sounded familiar to Clair—a song from her youth—entrancing and bittersweet.

Hudson rubbed his chin, looking bemused as if he were trying to think of something else to say.

Clair thought she should help him out. "I work down the street from you. At—"

Suddenly, a burly man in hippie attire bolted over to them. He looked as out of place as Clair felt. "Hey, I thought that was you," the fellow said to Hudson. "Do you remember me? I'm your old college roommate, Nathan Taylor." He gave Hudson a scrunching hug.

Their manly embrace looked painful to Clair, but she was far from familiar with male customs. She decided to give the two friends some time to themselves, so she backed away.

As Clair headed in the direction of the punch bowl, her muse about Hudson intensified. A twinge of pain came over her, along with exhilaration. How could it be? She'd never felt so wistful and yet so consciously alive—so forlorn and yet astonished. *Have I just met the desire of my heart? Dear Lord, I wish, oh how I wish. . .*

When she arrived at the punch table, Clair accepted a cup of the foamy pink drink. "Thank you." She took a sip then turned back to indulge in one more secret glimpse of the man who occupied her thoughts. She nearly dropped her cup as Hudson emerged from the crowd and marched right toward her.

three

Hudson strode up to Clair, hoping he didn't look too red-faced. "Hello again."

"Hi." Clair's face lit up.

He offered up a shrug. "You were welcome to stay and visit back there."

"I didn't want to interrupt. . .your reunion."

Hudson was relieved she didn't seem upset in the least. "Turned out, he wasn't my roommate. He had me confused with somebody else."

"Really?" She fiddled with her empty cup.

Now that Clair was standing in front of him, he was speechless. He pointed at her cup. "Is that stuff good?" *Oh brother. That was deep.*

"Yes, it's some kind of pink minty foam."

He grinned at her. "Sounds awful."

Clair laughed. "Not really."

"I'll give it a try." Hudson picked up a full cup off the table and drank it straight down. *Oh. Wow.* He tried hard not to make the revolting expression his taste buds demanded. The stuff tasted like nausea medicine. What was his sister thinking?

Clair pointed to her lip and smiled. "You have a little pink mustache." She offered Hudson a napkin.

For a second their hands touched in midair. If he'd known how to make the moment last longer, he would have made it happen. *I'll drink three more cups if she'll keep handing me napkins*. In fact, he knew he'd be willing to drink every drop in the bowl just to be near her. And he wasn't even sure why.

Clair held her cup over to the server, and the man refilled it up to the brim. Clair gave Hudson a shy smile as she sipped off a bit of the foam.

Now Clair had a cute little mustache, so he handed her a napkin from the table. Inside the haze of Hudson's romantic inclinations for Clair, he heard a woman's voice calling his name. He turned and realization set in. *It's Nona.*

"I'm sorry," he whispered to Clair. "I really wish I could stay longer, but I need to go." He let out a lingering sigh. "I gave someone a ride this evening. Nona. She's a friend of a friend who wanted to meet Leslie. *And* I promised her I'd introduce her around at the party."

Clair glanced over in Nona's direction. "That was very kind of you."

Hudson wished he hadn't been so kind. He'd like to get to know Clair better and take her out for coffee later. But duty called.

Clair set her cup down and looked at him. "I understand."

I think she really does. Hudson turned to go, and then stopped. *I don't want to walk away. I'll never see her again.* "Where did you say you worked?" He backed away from Clair without taking his eyes off her.

"Ima's Bookshop."

"I know the one. Just down the street from me." He smiled. "Maybe we could. . ." *No, don't say it. Not yet.* "Take care."

"I will." Clair's gaze shifted to the ground.

"Later then." He paused one more time to take in her sweet face, and then headed over to the bouncing and waving Nona.

❧

Clair's shoulder's sagged as she watched Hudson maneuver

through the cluster of guests. Why did her heart ache as he disappeared through the crowd? Had she thought, even for a moment, he might have been working up the courage to ask her out on a date? Would she have said yes?

She felt foolish standing there pining away, so she switched her attention to an exit she hadn't noticed before. With renewed vigor and swift steps, she made her way through the double doors, past the main entry hall, and outside into the cool night air.

To catch her breath, Clair stopped for a moment and leaned against an iron railing. People all dressed up in shimmering gowns and tuxedos glided by her and into the hotel. *Guess I'm a plain sparrow fluttering among a flock of doves.* She chuckled.

Clair filled her lungs with the late March air. A fresh breeze sweetened the night, feeling like silk against her skin. She suddenly thought of everyone gawking at her while she was sprawled across the floor. *It will be enough disgrace to last me for years.* She sighed.

But Hudson and his kind spirit would linger in her mind much longer than the embarrassment. She opened her hand to look at the gum he'd given her. She unwrapped it leisurely, rolled it up into a wad, and stuffed it in her mouth. Juicy. Spicy. Sweet. Hudson was right. Chewing the gum did calm her.

Clair noticed a couple getting into a black limousine, but she knew she couldn't even afford a taxi. The hike home was several blocks, but she was used to walking, though not necessarily under the shadows of the evening.

So, Clair glanced back once more, and then headed down the sidewalk, wishing all the while she could afford to fix her car. As she crossed the street at the first available stoplight, she prayed the Lord would protect her every step of the way. Then she focused on the sidewalk, doing all she could to avoid the eyes of passersby.

After a few minutes, the darkness felt like a heavy wool blanket, closing in around her. A shiver ran down Clair's spine as the night's shadows seemed to swallow her whole. She quoted a familiar scripture, seeking God's protective hand as she inched her way along. " 'Even though I walk through the valley of the shadow of death, I will fear no evil. . .' " Somehow just whispering the words from the psalm brought comfort.

Suddenly, from out of the cover of night, a white stretch limo cruised up next to her. Clair's heart quickened, and she kept watch on the vehicle as she picked up her pace.

One of the heavily tinted windows rolled down, revealing a man in a suit.

Clair couldn't see his face. She strode away from the limo. Her heels clatter-clomped on the concrete as if to keep time with her racing heartbeat.

"Don't be afraid. Glenn to your rescue here."

She stopped, relieved to hear a voice she recognized. As she turned and caught a glimpse of Glenn's face, Clair's fears dissipated. "But why are you following me?"

Glenn leaned outside the window. "I must confess I came looking for you because I was worried."

"Ah." *He must've seen my fall.*

"You disappeared like Houdini." He flashed a rehearsed pout.

"Sorry. I guess I should have said good-bye."

"But I thought you were having a good time."

She shrugged and glanced around, slightly unnerved by the sound of approaching footsteps. "A little."

"I want to drive you home. I feel responsible somehow."

"Why?" Clair wasn't sure what to think of his attentions. People, especially men, rarely even noticed her.

"I don't know," Glenn said. "Maybe because I talked you into something you didn't really want to do."

Clair started walking again, slowly. "I. . .can't let you take me home." Through the shadows, a couple of men passed her by. She tried to remain focused on the sidewalk, tried not to be afraid. *Even though I walk through the valley of the shadow. . .*

"And can you please tell me why?" Glenn gestured with his hand.

The limo crept along with her as she walked. "Because I don't know you. . .very well."

"Oh." Glenn chuckled. "That makes sense. But I promise you I'm a fine Christian man." He leaned back inside. "Drew, my man, tell this young lady what a great Christian guy I am."

The front window rolled down. The chauffeur tipped his hat back. "Good evening, miss."

"Hi."

"I've known Glenn a long time," Drew said. "He's a good guy. Cheap as a used toothpick sometimes, but—"

"Marvelous." Glenn frowned. "Thanks."

"You're welcome, sir," Drew replied with a grin.

Glenn peered out the window, donning a beseeching look. *He's trying to soften me up.* "I'm not sure."

Off in the distance, a man stepped out of the shadows and leaned against a light pole. He took a long drink from something hidden inside a paper bag then glanced Clair's way. A shiver ran down her spine as the stranger staggered toward her.

She gasped and turned toward the limo. "Yes please. Help!"

four

The limo lurched to a halt. Drew jumped out and opened the back door for Clair.

She scooted inside the car and gripped her hands on the seat. "Please lock the—"

The moment he slipped back inside, all the doors locked soundly.

Clair let out a breath of air. *Safe.* After she'd calmed down, she told them her address.

The stranger, just outside their window, spewed obscenities at them. He reminded Clair of a mangy dog she'd befriended once on the playground at school, but all she could safely do now was send up a prayer for him and one of thanksgiving that she hadn't been hurt.

In spite of her relief, Clair stayed near the door handle. Even though Glenn had a consoling smile and she felt grateful for his help, he still seemed an imposing figure.

Once the car shifted back into gear and they pulled away, Glenn turned to her. "If you get any closer to that door handle, you'll make Drew think you're about to jump ship." Drew laughed, and Glenn added, "I promise. . .you have nothing to be afraid of in here."

Clair nodded then glanced back toward the street as the man disappeared from view.

"Looked like a scary guy," Glenn observed. "I don't even want to think about what could have happened to you back there."

He seemed concerned. She stopped chewing her gum and shifted it to the inside of her cheek as she explained. "My car—it needs a new transmission. That's why I was walking."

Glenn lowered his voice. "Well, taking a cab is always an option."

How much should she reveal about her financial situation? Glenn would soon see her modest home, so he might as well know all of it. "I needed the money for my. . .electric bill next month."

"I shouldn't be pressuring answers out of you. I apologize." Glenn appeared perplexed. He drummed his fingers on a book sitting between them.

Clair glanced down to discover a leather-bound Bible. She relaxed and let go of some of her fears. *For you are with me; your rod and your staff, they comfort me.*

She glanced around, taking note of the limo's interior—the creamy leather, the romantic lighting, and the soft swirling jazz. So luxurious. Like a miniature palace on wheels. So unlike the surroundings she'd grown used to. She gave her gum a few more chews, but it'd become tasteless and stiff. When she thought Glenn wouldn't notice, she slipped the little round ball back into its wrapper.

Glenn held out his hand in front of her.

Oh dear. He'd noticed the gum. Had she been smacking? Clair could feel her eyes widen and her skin color all the way down to her toes. She gingerly placed the wrapped gum into his palm. "Thank you," she whispered.

"My pleasure." He disposed of it then flipped open a leather-covered lid. Inside were sodas and sparkling water on ice. "Would you like something to drink?"

Clair shook her head.

"I'm curious about your job." Glenn took a Perrier from the

cooler. "You said you work at Ima's Bookshop in the River Market District?"

"Yes. I work for Ima Langston. She owns the bookshop. I stock the shelves and help with the paperwork."

"And is that what you want to do with your life?" He poured his drink into a glass.

Clair ventured a glance in his direction. His double-breasted suit framed an elegant build, and his silky dark curls softened his extravagant exterior. "Ima is. . .good to me. So it would be unkind if I left her now. She needs me."

"But if you could do anything, what would it be?" He took a sip of his beverage.

She twisted her wrist against her leg. A babyish habit, but somehow it gave her comfort when life got too exhausting. Or when questions got too probing. "I suppose I want to. . . own a bookstore someday. I guess. But that would mean I'd have to deal more with. . .customers and employees. It's a people kind of business, but I'm a. . ."

"You're a what?" Glenn's tone came off gentle but concerned.

"It's not easy for me to talk about." A stillness settled around them. The quiet seemed to last an eternity to Clair.

A few moments later, Drew pulled up in front of her house.

"Thank you. . .for bringing me home." Clair felt self-conscious about the shabbiness of her small home—the peeling gray paint and the broken sidewalk that led up to the front porch. But she certainly couldn't change anything now. *If only I'd had enough money to plant some tulips.*

"Yes, of course." Glenn's expression changed from buoyancy to pensiveness as he looked beyond her toward the little house. His window motored down halfway and then he gripped the glass. "It was my pleasure." He stared at her home in silence then turned to take in the rest of the street.

Was he shocked at the ramshackle cheerlessness of it? Or was he not feeling well?

Glenn turned back to her with the oddest look on his face, one she couldn't interpret. Then he reached to take her hand, wide-eyed. "Clair, before you go. . ."

"Yes?"

"I. . .I feel a prompting from the Lord to help you."

"Help me?" Clair felt more confused than ever.

Glenn looked just beyond her face. A flicker of something distant and forlorn passed through his expression. "I remember a time when I could barely speak in front of anyone, let alone a crowd. I was the kid at the back of the room, petrified of my own shadow."

Glenn seemed to wait for her reaction. What could she say? Confidence and charisma seemed to mark his every move and word. He spoke so well, he could surely command a room full of people with a mere wave of his hand. It was difficult for her to imagine him as a quiet, frightened boy. "You seem. . . fearless." She felt her cheeks warm.

"Cocky is a better word," Drew called from the driver's seat.

Glenn chortled. "Thanks, old buddy. You're killing me here." He pushed a button. Drew rolled his eyes and grinned as the glass enclosed them in a cocoon of privacy.

"Many years ago, someone offered me some help and I took it. I was then able to pull myself up from some pretty rough circumstances." He smoothed his tie. "Now I teach people how to present themselves in their business and private worlds."

Clair squeezed her hands so tightly she could feel her heartbeat in her fingers. "But I can't afford your help." Surely he could tell that by looking at her home.

"Please let me explain. This man, Walter Sullivan, gave

me the leg up with one condition. He wanted me to pass the help on to someone else once I'd succeeded in my profession. I'm embarrassed to say I'd totally forgotten my promise to Walter, until I saw you tonight."

Clair put her hand to her cheek. "I've always been. . .shy. But I guess I didn't realize how pitiful I looked."

"No. Not at all." Glenn turned toward her and smiled. "You, Clair O'Neal, are a gift from heaven this earth has yet to open."

She met his gaze. His hazel eyes appeared so startling and inquisitive, she looked away. *Why would he say such a thing? He doesn't even know me.*

Glenn cleared his throat. "I didn't mention it earlier, but I did see you fall."

Clair cringed. "I was afraid of that."

"Yes. I almost made it to you in time, but I saw Leslie's brother, Hudson, come to your aid." Glenn turned away. "Then later, I couldn't find you."

"You saw me fall. . .and you *still* want to help me?"

"I'm certain I do." Glenn reached out his hand but then drew it back. "But not as a client. As a friend." He appeared to study her expression. "Please understand me. I mean this offer within a totally professional context. But I want to handle it as Walter did—as a friend. I know you don't know me. And all this must seem strange to you"—he turned once more to glance at her house—"but I can assure you I've never been more serious in my life."

Clair looked at her hands, intertwined like a knotted rope. "I want to be. . .less bashful? It makes me feel so. . ."

"Caged and helpless?" Glenn finished.

"Yes. Sometimes." She turned away to the window again, embarrassed to be speaking of such intimate matters with a person she'd just met. Then again, perhaps the Lord had sent Glenn Yves to her as a gift—to push her beyond the insecurities that had held her bound for so many years, to rid her of the unspoken doubts and fears.

"I believe I can help."

Oh Lord, I'm ready, if this is Your timing. I've walked this road for so long.

Clair's palms perspired again. Could she truly find a way out of the lonely place she'd known since childhood? It seemed impossible, but maybe the words of her stepfather had been untrue. Perhaps she wasn't a misfit. She suddenly imagined herself doing some of the things she'd dreamed of—waiting on customers at the bookshop, joining the women's group at church, and maybe even helping needy kids.

Clair had no idea how the Lord might use Glenn to bring about such miracles, but saying no to such a generous offer seemed unwise. She summoned her courage to look at him. Compassion filled his eyes, yet something else lingered in his smile. A glimmer she couldn't read. No matter how kind he appeared, she would keep her caution within reach.

"Yes," Clair said softly, "I guess you'll be Dr. Frankenstein, and I will be your monster."

five

Glenn threw his head back and laughed.

Clair was pleased to make him laugh, but in spite of the sudden camaraderie, she felt grateful all had been made clear. Glenn would simply be fulfilling a promise. Besides, the thought of any romantic interest with him was beyond silly. Even if he could help her with her timidity, she would still be one of "the invisibles," and he, one of "the beautifuls." Clair felt her face getting warm just knowing what she'd say next. "Will you be able to help me stop. . .blushing?"

"Now why would I want to do that?" Glenn rested back on the soft leather seat. "It's an endearing quality. People rarely blush anymore. Most people have seen and heard too much, I suppose."

"But it makes me feel. . .like a child."

"No, you're just unassuming and meek. And if this book is true"—he rested his hand on the Bible—"the meek do not go unblessed."

"True," she whispered.

He glanced at her house once more then turned back, giving her a warm smile. "I do believe we were meant to meet tonight, Clair. Surely the Lord had a hand in this."

"Do you think?"

"I do." He kissed the back of her hand and whispered, "But it is late, and I don't want to keep you."

"Thank you so much for the ride. And. . .for your offer to help me."

"You're welcome." He released her hand. "Good night, Clair. We'll wait until you're snugly inside before we go. And in the next week or so, I'll drop by your bookshop." He smiled at her.

"Good-bye." Like a coach's door in a fairytale, Clair's door magically opened.

Drew stood near, uniformed and dignified, but he smiled, tipping his hat at her. "Take care."

She thanked him and then took long strides up the path. As she approached her front door, she remembered leaving her evening bag in the hotel. *Oh no! How could I have done that?* Clair reproached herself and reached under the planter for the extra key, trying to recall the contents of her thrift store purse. A house key, a peppermint, Ima's business card, a plastic comb. . . Whoever discovered the bag would certainly be unimpressed. But what else would the person find? Ah yes. Her driver's license. Surely that would help in the recovery process.

Clair turned back around to the street, noticing that Glenn and Drew still waited in the limo. She raised her hand in a wave and then slipped through the front door. Clair made her way through her musty house with the glow from a clear moon. Except for the eternal ticking of a wall clock, she noted what a cave-like space welcomed her home. Eager to see, she flicked the switch.

Lighted flooded her small abode.

As she turned, Clair caught her reflection in a wall mirror— thick eyebrows, forlorn brown eyes, and shoulder-length, mousy dark hair that hadn't had a real beauty shop cut in five years. And yet just this evening, Glenn had referred to her as beautiful. *Hmm.* She leaned in a bit closer, looking for some sort of hidden treasure. She would have to remember to look up *beautiful* in the dictionary. Surely the meaning had been updated to read, "Plain as a mayonnaise sandwich."

The wall clock came to life. Eight chimes. *I'm probably the only twenty-first-century female who ever left a party before nine o'clock. Oh well. There are worse things to be known for.*

Clair gave up on her image and headed to the kitchen. She looked around at the existence she'd created for herself, which was now illuminated by the harsh florescent lights. Clumps of flowers, dried from her backyard, hung upside down over the sink, faded and lifeless. The rest of the kitchen was almost bare except for a table and chairs. *Not too appealing.* Clair wondered if Glenn could help her be a bit more light and merry. *How lovely that would be.*

Just before bed, Clair settled into her worn but comfortable chair with a cup of chamomile tea and a novel. Dear Ima allowed her to read any of the books in the shop as long as she didn't bend the pages, but even the latest hot-off-the-press Christian novel couldn't keep her thoughts from whirling off, playing the night's events over and over in her mind. Especially the moments with Hudson. What a wonderful addition he had been to an otherwise nerve-wracking night. His eyes, filled with kindness. The sound of his voice bringing comfort. The touch of his hand as he reached to help her.

Yes, the Lord had surely sent Hudson at just the right time. She sighed as she pondered it all. So much to take in. Years had gone by in her life with less activity than she'd known in one brief evening. Clearly, the Lord was at work. There was no denying it.

And what about Glenn? She wouldn't lay aside the idea that his offer of help might be linked to the stirring hand of God, also. Could it be it wasn't too late for something wonderful to happen in her life?

Clair bit her lower lip, forcing herself not to cry. There had been too much sorrow in her childhood, more than any little girl deserved. But now hope had come near—a brand-new emotion. And that hope gave her courage to believe the impossible.

Yes, surely the Lord had orchestrated this evening's events—in preparation for something more, perhaps? *He restores my soul.* The psalm continued to run through her mind, bringing assurance and a sense of overwhelming peace.

Clair set the book down on her lap and began to sing a familiar worship song, a joy she'd known in solitude for as long as she could remember. Like a reassuring hug, she let the words soothe and encourage her.

Bedtime arrived, but sleep did not come easily for Clair. She stared out into the moonlit night, thinking and praying.

෨

After a restless sleep, Clair rose later than usual. She hurried to get dressed, anxious to see if Ima was feeling better. She put on her best wool slacks and pullover sweater and began her walk to the bookshop.

In spite of the budding trees and smell of spring, the weather had turned frosty overnight. The chilling breeze seeped through her coat, so Clair snuggled her hands down into her pockets and walked more briskly toward the river.

For a brief moment, the street emptied of cars and an unearthly quiet settled over her spirit. Music—a familiar friend—began to play in her head, first as if from far away and then louder and clearer. As Clair strode along the sidewalk, she sang the tune softly to herself. *Ah yes.* Sweet and stirring, like a fragrant zephyr. The song was a favorite from her past and the very same melody Hudson had hummed at the party.

Looking both ways, she trotted across the street toward the bookshop. Clair had always admired Ima's storefront. The red brick facade and the antique sign made the shop quaint and appealing. The benches and black lampposts along the avenue also gave the area a charming look. A streetcar suddenly rolled by on its tracks, and Clair couldn't help but smile as she noted the smiling tourists inside. She loved all of the old-fashioned elements of her fair city. They brought a familiar comfort. If only she had been born in a different era, a time when quiet, reserved women were the norm instead of an anomaly. Yes, she would surely have made a fine character in a nineteenth-century tale.

Thinking of books reminded Clair to stop dreaming and check on Ima. She pulled out her key, opened the door, and listened to the familiar jangle of the bell. How she had grown to love the sound. It meant she'd entered the kind and comforting world of Ima and her treasures.

Clair closed the door. "Ima." She glanced down at the chair where Ima always tossed her purse. There it sat, reassuring her that all was well. Clair breathed in the smell of peppermint. Her employer liked to keep lots of potpourri around the shop in little terra-cotta bowls. The soothing fragrance along with the soft chairs and oak shelves made the Christian bookshop cozy and inviting. Ima had wanted the store to be like home, and the customers loved it.

The metal bell above the door jangled again. Clair turned to discover Hudson Mandel standing in the doorway. She could hardly believe it. Her heart pounded faster at the sight of him, and she couldn't seem to hide the smile that rose up.

"Hi," he said.

Clair smiled and tried to still her thumping heart. "Hello."

"Something smells good." Hudson cleared his throat. "Well, I. . .uh. . .came by to give you this." He eased her evening bag from his coat pocket and set it down on the counter as if it were an heirloom.

She slipped her coat off. "Thank you." Clair felt a little dismayed, wishing the purse hadn't been the reason he'd dropped by.

Their eyes met. Clair realized it hadn't been something she'd made up in her mind. Hudson really *did* have the warmest, darkest brown eyes she'd ever seen.

After staring at each other for an immeasurable amount of time, Clair moved her gaze to a row of empty shelves. Her thoughts shifted to the changes Ima wanted to make in the bookshop. *Ima?* She still hadn't heard her employer make any noises in the back room. "I'm sorry. But I need to check on Ima. She hasn't been feeling well lately."

"Don't let me keep you. But I don't mind waiting." He removed his coat. "I wanted to ask you something."

Ask me something? Clair blushed. "I'll only be a moment." She made her way toward the back room, stepping around boxes stacked in the hallway. She glanced toward the ladies' room. Open and lights off. "Ima? Are you okay?" When Clair heard no answer, she felt a quickening of her heart. She hurried to the tiny kitchen, panic engulfing her as she saw Ima, pale and lifeless on the floor.

"No!" Clair grabbed onto the doorframe to steady herself. She wanted to scream, but only a sob escaped. Her head went dizzy. Clair willed herself to stay conscious as she knelt next to Ima and placed her finger on the side of her neck. No pulse. "Ima, can you hear me?" Should she try to do CPR or call 911? Clair heard a ringing in her ears, and she felt like she was moving through a tunnel. *I cannot pass out! Lord, please help me.*

Hudson burst into the room. "Clair, what happened?" Without waiting for an answer, he rushed to Ima's side.

six

"Call 911!" Hudson tilted Ima's head back and put his ear to the woman's mouth to listen and feel for her breath. Nothing. He pressed his finger to her neck. No pulse. *Oh God, help this woman.*

Clair stood frozen, the color draining from her face.

"We need to call 911!"

"Yes." Clair staggered to her feet and grabbed the phone on the wall.

Hudson stared at Ima. No breathing. No pulse. He knew he'd have to do CPR. Was it ten compressions or fifteen? *Quick, think, man.* He started the compressions. "One. Two. Three." He continued to count to fifteen. He blew into Ima's mouth two times, hoping he was right.

Clair knelt down opposite Hudson, still clutching the phone. "They're coming," she said, "but they've asked me to stay on the line. D–do you feel any heartbeat?"

Hudson felt for a pulse again and watched Ima's chest for movement. Nothing.

"She has to be okay," Clair whispered. "She has to be. Oh please, dear God. . ."

Ima remained unresponsive, and her skin felt cool like marble. Unnaturally cool. Hudson feared she'd already gone. He kept up the CPR. After a moment, he glanced up. Clair's eyes had that faraway look again. "You okay?"

"Yes." She continued to grip the phone.

"Count with me."

Clair's mouth eased open, but no words came out.

"Are you with me?"

She caught his gaze and nodded.

"Come on," Hudson said. "Five, six, seven, eight, nine. . ."

Clair began counting along with him.

After a few more minutes, Hudson could hear the sirens. "They're here."

"I'll go." Clair passed on the information to the person on the other end of the phone line, then ended the call. She scrambled up off the floor and ran out of the room.

The wail of the sirens grew louder until Hudson heard voices at the front of the store. Immediately paramedics surrounded him. He stepped away from Ima. "She's not breathing, and I can't find a heartbeat."

Clair's eyes rolled back as she slumped against the wall.

Hudson caught her before she fell to the floor. He swept her up in his arms and took her from the room.

"Do you need some help?" one of the paramedics yelled to him.

"She's fainted, but I think she'll be okay." Hudson noticed the store's tiny back office, just a few feet from where he now stood, and began to move in that direction. *A couch.* With care, he eased Clair down onto the cushions.

He snatched some paper towels from the bathroom and ran some cold water. He glanced through the door.

One paramedic pulled out what looked like defibrillator paddles.

Once back at Clair's side, Hudson brushed her hair away from her face and dabbed the damp towels on her forehead and began to pray. The morning certainly hadn't gone as planned, but somehow he knew he was in the right place. Surely the Lord had led him here so that Clair wouldn't have to face this alone.

Just then, she let out a puff of air and released a faint moan.

He took hold of her hand. "Clair?"

Her eyes fluttered open.

Hudson smiled. *Thank You, Lord.* He squeezed her hand, noticing how fragile it felt and yet how warm.

"What happened?" Clair took in a deep breath.

"You're okay. You just fainted."

"Ima." She looked over his shoulder with wide eyes. "I've got to help her. Is she okay now?"

"I think they're about to put her on the gurney. She'll be on her way soon."

"I want to go with her." Clair clasped the sleeve of his coat.

She had the most earnest look on her face, he wanted to take her into his arms and tell her all would be well. But he knew he couldn't make that promise, and noting Clair's shyness, a hug would more likely shock her than comfort her. "I doubt they'll let us go with them, but I'm sure we can follow the ambulance."

"You don't have to take me. I'll call a taxi."

"I'm glad to do it."

"It's the second time," Clair whispered.

"Second time for what?"

"I keep falling," she said. "And you keep picking me up."

He smiled at her.

"I'm all right now." She rubbed her head as she rose to a sitting position.

Hudson helped her off the couch and then held her until she was steady on her feet.

They made their way back out into the store, watching as the paramedics lifted Ima's body onto a stretcher and wheeled it out the front door. All the while, Clair stood in silence, her face pale.

Once the ambulance pulled away, Hudson again offered to drive her to the hospital. She agreed this time then locked up the store and hurried with him to his pickup truck.

A chilling wind whipped their clothes as Hudson opened the door for her and helped her inside. He glanced upward, noting the clouds and the approaching storm. He ran to the driver's side, scooted in under the wheel, and followed the flashing lights and sirens down the freeway.

Hudson caught a glimpse of Clair as he turned the corner. She sat still and lovely like a pale rose. *Is she afraid for Ima or afraid of me?* They'd only just met the evening before, so it was possible she didn't fully trust him yet. But he couldn't have felt more different. Somehow, he not only trusted her, he felt an immediate connection.

Then the thought of her soft sweater against his skin came to mind. *I need to keep my wits.* Hudson gave the steering wheel a white-knuckled grip to concentrate on his driving. "You okay?"

Clair nodded as she stared down at her hands, which were folded together like a little nest.

Perhaps she was already grieving for her employer, thinking as he did that Ima had already passed away. He wanted to console Clair but wasn't sure how. He'd always been better expressing emotion through his lyrics than his lips. *Wish I could fix that someday.*

Minutes later, they pulled into the emergency parking at St. John Medical Center. Once they were inside, a nurse asked them to sit in the waiting room. They made their way through the starkly lit room, amidst the smell of disinfectant and the throng of people.

Clair finally chose a string of empty molded seats in the corner by the snack machines. Hudson slid in next to her. The chairs felt hard and unforgiving, so he leaned forward with his elbows on his knees. He made another appeal to the Almighty to spare Ima, but he knew her life would have to be left in His hands.

Clair rose and paced back and forth, her arms hugging her waist. She hummed ever so faintly.

The minutes drifted on and on as they waited for news of Ima. Hudson shifted to find a more comfortable position. *What a miserable little seat.* He rubbed his hands along the legs of his jeans and noticed a stack of magazines. The entire heap, though, appeared to be for women. *Great.* After he'd flipped through and read all he could stand on menopause and fashion tips, he slipped the magazine back into its pile for some other lucky guy to digest.

He glanced over at Clair. She stood near the soda machine with her eyes closed. He couldn't tell if she was praying or just resting her eyes. He realized she might want something to drink, so he pulled out his wallet.

A man strode up to them wearing a white jacket and a grave smile—a smile that surely revealed the truth of Ima's fate. He introduced himself as Dr. Milburn.

"I'm sorry to have to tell you this. . ." he started. His gaze shifted down to the ground, then back up again, as he spoke in a low voice, "Your friend. . .I'm afraid she didn't make it."

Clair shook her head, and a look of disbelief came over her.

The doctor gave her a sympathetic look as he explained. "She died of heart failure."

Clair's trembling hand covered her mouth. She blinked a few times, but no tears filled her eyes.

Hudson ached to reach out to her but felt he should wait

for a sign that his comfort might be needed. No sign came, so he just stood near her.

Moments later, they were whisked off into the administrative office. Clair answered all their questions, giving them information about Ima's sister in Pine Bluff.

After Clair viewed Ima's body once more, Hudson waited for her just outside the door. When she came out, he gently placed his hand on her back and steered her through the clusters of people who waited with their own heartbreaks and hopes.

When they reached the foyer, Clair said, "I'll call for a taxi. Thank you. . .for everything. You've been so kind. How can I ever—"

"Please let me drive you home or back to the store." He studied her expression. Her large brown eyes took him in yet still kept him at a distance.

Clair glanced away. "Why are you helping me?"

"Well, you're a fellow human being, and you need help." That was all true. But why couldn't he be bold enough to say the rest? *Probably because she'd think I was certifiable.*

Truth was he liked her, even though they'd barely met. In fact, Clair seemed to be just like the woman he'd written about in one of his songs—a young woman who was a little misplaced in the world, yet so full of goodness. He'd never known a woman like Clair could really exist beyond his own imagination. *But she's standing right in front of me.* He thought of her anguish again. *I better not push.* He knew grief had to be a personal journey.

Clair's gaze slowly met his. "Okay." She nodded. "You may drive me back to the bookshop."

Hudson felt so pleased with her answer he wanted to embrace her. *Not good. I just need to calm down.*

Later as he drove Clair back to the store, Hudson considered grief and all its revelations. A person's disposition certainly seemed easier to discern while under fire. Based on all he had seen thus far, Clair had a strong and steady faith. Hudson recalled his own response to his uncle's sudden heart attack, and how he'd allowed his mind to become coated with a dark layer of doubts about God. Fortunately, over time, he'd been able to rise above the uncertainties, but it wasn't easy.

He wondered what Clair's haunts—the word he always used for the things that bugged people—were. Their weakest links. Everyone had them. Even Christians.

Once Hudson had Clair safely back at the shop, he caught himself gazing at her just as he had that very morning. Fortunately, the color had come back to her face, but the sadness in her eyes tore at his heart.

He glanced around the bookshelves so he wouldn't be caught gawking at her. He hadn't noticed before, but many of the bookshelves were empty, and stacks of boxes sat near the counter. It looked like they were about to restock. On the wall just above Clair's head were all kinds of hats—a fedora, a derby, a sombrero, and even a green beanie cap with a little red propeller on top.

Hudson coughed since he couldn't think of anything to say. Should he ask her out for coffee at the shop down the street? Would she consider him the worst kind of jerk under the circumstances, or would she welcome the company? *In a second or two, you'll have to either say something or leave. Just open your mouth.*

seven

Instinct told Hudson the moment wasn't right to ask her for what she might consider a date, even though he longed to help Clair deal with her grief. "I guess I'll go. Let me know if you need anything."

"Okay." Clair seemed to look at everything in the store but him.

Hudson shuffled his feet, thinking he must look more like a squirming child than a man. "If you need anything at all. . ." *Anything. I'm here.*

She nodded.

He opened the door of the shop and turned once more to Clair. If the bookshop were to close now, he might never see her again. The very idea tore at his heart. "I'd certainly like to take you out for some coffee."

Clair suddenly looked surprised. Maybe shocked was a better word.

"I would like to, but under the circumstances, I'd better not," Clair said. "But thank you."

Hudson's mouth flew open. *I was mumbling out loud again? Oh brother.* "What did I say. . .exactly?"

Clair blushed. "You said you'd like to take me out for some coffee."

"I have this habit of just saying what's in my head. Sorry." Hudson wondered what else he'd said. Should he offer to go with her to Ima's funeral? Maybe he'd better leave before she knew he was a total fool. "Bye. Be careful now."

"Bye."

Without humiliating himself further, Hudson waved and eased out the door. He could have kicked himself for putting his needs first. *What was I thinking?*

Walking back toward his shop, he reached another impasse in his mind. If he wanted to ask Clair out on a date, he'd have to dredge up his persuasive skills again.

But then there was also the issue of Tara Williamson. His family and Tara's folks had indeed known each other since the origin of dirt, but even with the manipulative efforts of her family and his sister, he and Tara had only dated a little on and off. Mostly as friends. In spite of all the facts, when it came to Tara and matrimony, he still felt the pressure.

A car honked, jerking Hudson from his thoughts. He stuffed his hands in the pockets of his coat. Even with his long-sleeved shirt and heavy coat, the air still felt cold to him. Maybe he'd have a hot cup of coffee anyway. *Darrell can handle the guitar shop for a bit. I need some time to think.* A steaming mug of coffee sounded good, even if he had to drink it alone.

&

A couple of weeks later, Clair stood in front of Ima's Bookshop, key in hand. She hesitated to enter, focusing instead on the truth of her new situation. *How can it be that I now own this bookshop?* Just as she slipped the key in the lock, she heard a voice calling her name.

Glenn Yves, in all his dazzling glory, strode up to her. With his black suit and lofty frame, all he lacked was a sword and horse. He reminded her of the daring heroes in medieval novels who slew dragons. But then again, she never went out. She had no point of reference concerning men. *Perhaps I embellish them in my mind.*

Glenn touched her arm as if she were his dearest friend. "How are you, Clair?"

His sudden closeness made her catch her breath. But he didn't laugh at her childishness. He just looked at her with those startling hazel eyes of his. Clair stared down at his hand, which was still in contact with her arm. She had yet to get used to people touching her.

He removed his hand but not his gaze. "You've lost some of your rosy glow. Are you all right?"

"I'm just. . .surprised to see you."

"I know it's been a while, but I've come to honor my promise. How about lunch at the River Grill? We can begin our quest."

"I'm sorry." Clair wished she could say yes. "It just that. . .I can't afford to eat there."

Glenn waved his hand. "No, no. I'm buying."

"But I can't accept—"

"You haven't changed your mind about my offer." He leaned down to catch her gaze. "Have you?"

Clair clutched her purse in her hands, twisting the top back and forth, trying to rev up some courage. She'd need his help now more than ever. If she were to run the bookshop, learning to deal with customers would be vital. She had no real excuse to suddenly change her mind, except for barely knowing this man whose intense look almost swallowed her whole. "But I never expected our sessions to include lunch."

"I usually meet my clients at my office, but I thought a casual atmosphere might be more to your liking." He gestured with open palms. "Less intimidating."

Clair stared down at her threadbare dress and worn-out shoes with dismay. "I'm not really dressed for—"

He shook his head. "It doesn't matter. All of that will be

taken care of. . .later." He gave her an encouraging smile. "So, what do you say? Will you let me change your world?"

Clair let out a long breath of air, wondering what he meant. She knew almost any small improvement in her life would be welcome, but she still couldn't figure out why such a savvy and sophisticated man would be interested in helping her. Then she remembered Glenn's promise to Walter Sullivan, who'd reached out to help him years before. *He will surely tire of me, but in the meantime I may learn something that could help me run the bookshop. I will do it for Ima.* "Okay. Change your world. I mean. . .*my* world." Clair reddened at her blunder.

"Who knows, Ms. O'Neal," Glenn said. "You may very well change *my* world. Yes indeed." He flashed his straight white teeth at her—like ivories on a grand piano.

Clair smiled back at him, covering her mouth with her hand. She hadn't liked her smile since grade school. Too peculiar—it didn't fit her face.

"It's really nice out today. Want to take a walk?" He took her elbow, and they glided forward. "By the way, you have a wonderful smile. No need to cover it up."

Oh dear. Clair strolled with him down the sidewalk. *I'm slumping again. Straighten up, Clair!*

Glenn cleared his throat. "The first piece of advice I have for you is to raise your head and pull back your shoulders. Stand tall. Think tall. You can practice as we walk. You're much too beautiful to droop like a faded flower."

He notices everything. Clair could feel her face getting warm as she drew herself up straight. But why had he called her beautiful? Was he making fun? She did her best to straighten her shoulders and raise her head as they walked toward the River Grill, but she felt self-conscious and embarrassed with her new posture, as if she were putting on airs.

Without warning, Clair tripped on a piece of uneven sidewalk. In her effort to catch herself, her hands slapped against the concrete.

"Clair!" Glenn took hold of her arms and lifted her up. "Are you all right?"

She nodded, feeling the wasp-like sting on her palms and feeling more like a fool than she ever had before. If that were possible. *Oh God, please help me. I'm a walking disaster.*

After taking a handkerchief from his pants pocket, Glenn gently wiped the dirt off her hands. In that one moment, he was indeed the hero, and he had just slain a thousand dragons for her. Clair straightened again and tried to smile. "I'm afraid I—"

"People trip all the time. I once tripped going up on stage to give a speech on 'Why Image Makes All the Difference.'"

"Really?"

"Does it get much worse than that?" He grinned.

"Did people laugh?" She couldn't imagine such a thing happening to one of "the beautifuls."

"Well, some of the people did. And then I laughed, which sort of gave permission for other people to chuckle. It certainly made a good icebreaker."

As Clair listened, she noticed two women batting their eyes at Glenn while they strolled by. Clair supposed that sort of thing happened to him often.

"I ended up using the accident as a teaching tool in my speech." He held the handkerchief out to her. "You may keep it."

"No. I—"

"Please, I insist."

Clair finally reached out and accepted his gift. The material felt expensive and sumptuous and was monogrammed with the gold initials G. Y. "Thank you." She eased the handkerchief into an inner pocket of her purse where she kept all objects of importance. She couldn't help but ponder Glenn's upbeat attitude. *If I'm around him long enough, will it rub off on me?*

Clair felt the sharp tingle from a pebble in her shoe. Why hadn't she felt that before? Humiliated enough for one day, she decided to just absorb the pain as they walked.

Moments later, after passing two souvenir shops, a bakery, a T-shirt shop, and a café, they were suddenly breezing by the River Front Guitar Shop. Clair turned her head for a glimpse through the window. She didn't expect to see Hudson, but she looked anyway. Funny how she'd strolled past that guitar store many times and had no idea who worked inside. *Hudson.* Would he ever come by the bookshop again?

After a few more strides, Clair could smell the mouth-watering scents wafting out the front door of the Arkansas River Grill. Relief. At least there'd be no more falling accidents.

When they stepped inside, the maitre d' promptly escorted them to an intimate table overlooking the Arkansas River. Sunlight played on the water, making rhinestone shimmers across the water. The table, decorated with white linen, floating candles, and a spray of orchids, appeared romantic in every way. *Like something out of a movie. But this certainly isn't a date, and it's not exactly casual. At least, not from what I can gather.*

A waiter removed Clair's napkin, fluffed it, and then snapped it in a theatrical gesture. He bent low, positioning the white cloth on her lap with precision.

You prepare a table before me. . . She bit her lower lip, trying not to allow a nervous giggle to slip out.

Then their very efficient waiter handed them their menus and mentioned the specials of the day.

Clair glanced around, absorbing the loveliness of the

restaurant. Her gaze stopped on a startling sight. She could barely believe her eyes. Hudson sat on the other side of the restaurant. He was with someone—someone fair-haired with straight shoulders and a confident air.

Clair wanted to hide behind something, but the menu wasn't big enough. Hudson deserved to be with a woman who could actually open her mouth and talk. And talk she most certainly did. In fact, Hudson's date appeared to be so blessed with copious amounts of talk and giggles that she drew the attention of the other patrons.

Then the woman's sudden burst of laughter drew Glenn's attention. He glanced across the room. "I don't know that chatty woman in black, but I do recognize the man with the blazer and. . .ahem. . .tennis shoes." He winced. "It's Leslie Mandel's brother, Hudson. Remember, you met him at the party."

"Yes."

Clair was glad Glenn wasn't looking at her, since a rush of heat had spread across her face. She touched the velvety petals of the orchid blossoms in an attempt to take her mind off who was sitting across the room.

"Well, looks like Hudson's got quite a live wire there." Glenn seemed amused. "Her shoes may be alligator, but her cackle is genuine hyena."

Clair wanted to laugh but held it in. Could a woman so beautiful actually have a flaw? Such an idea had never entered her mind before.

All of a sudden, Clair saw that Hudson noticed her from across the room. He waved, but his eyes were filled with surprise and confusion. She felt so discombobulated, all she could muster was a smile. She would need to turn her chair a bit more to the window to keep her mind on the matters at hand. Hudson was clearly with someone else anyway. Clair realized now she'd been childish to have gotten her hopes up concerning him, but then maybe Hudson wondered what she was doing here. . .with Glenn. *I hope he doesn't think we're dating.* She turned her attention back to the menu.

Glenn fingered his watch. He was wearing a wristwatch that looked just like the gold Rolex Clair had seen in a magazine ad. She'd never known anyone who could afford such luxury. She tried not to stare.

After they'd considered the menu and asked the waiter a few questions, Glenn ordered a filet mignon to be cooked rare, and Clair ordered the chicken cordon bleu since it appeared to be the least expensive thing on the menu.

When the waiter left, Clair eased back in her chair, gazing out at the Arkansas River, at the bluish-green colors and the smooth cool surface. The *toot* of a steamboat could be heard in the distance. She could picture it now, filled with tourists. A sailboat glided along the water, looking tranquil.

"I love strolling on the river trail." Clair let her mind play with happier times. "And I love all the bridges here. Most of all, I love the old-fashioned trolleys and the horse-drawn carriages." In truth, the remnants of days gone by seemed to suit her personality, though she wondered why she'd let herself ramble on about it in such a way.

"I especially love the older bridges. They have a lot of character." Glenn's words poured out as rich and smooth as a malted milk shake. "I'd love to hear what's been happening in your life."

Clair turned her attention back to his question. "Well, I. . . uh. . .Ima passed away."

"Oh no. So suddenly?"

"She'd been unwell for some time. Ima was a friend to me. My only friend." Clair wished she hadn't mentioned the last part. It sounded too bleak.

"I'm sorry," Glenn said. "When did she die?"

"The morning after the party. . .of heart failure."

Glenn touched her hand.

Remembering bits of the funeral, she sighed inside. The meager flowers, the solemn service, and the desperate expression on the face of Ima's sister—so forlorn and lost. The same way Clair felt inside.

"What will you do if the bookshop closes?" He released her hand.

"I. . .she. . .left the business to me. . .in her will."

"Now *that* is something." Glenn took a sip of his water.

She smiled, not wanting to tell him how much it grieved her to own the shop, how undeserving she felt to receive such a generous gift. She took a long drink of her water, wishing she could wash the thoughts away.

"I assume you'll keep it open, then."

"Yes, I plan to. And hopefully our customers will continue to frequent the shop. Ima always said people spend money on the things they truly love."

"And she loved books."

"Like they were her friends." Clair smiled. "Ima had plans to expand the bookstore."

As the conversation continued, Clair thought of Hudson again and glanced his way. *Oh my.* He'd risen from his chair and was walking toward her. She suddenly couldn't breathe.

Hudson approached her table. But when she looked at him, he halted mid-stride and stared at her with the most beseeching expression she'd ever seen. Everything around them—the talk and the clatter—all seemed suspended. Clair felt alone with Hudson just for a second as their gaze intensified. Then he veered toward an alcove of restrooms, and the moment dissolved as he went on his way. A rush of sound filled her ears again. What could it mean? Did he feel the same way she did? *If only Hudson would give me another chance, I would say yes!*

"Ima's plan could be a smart business move." Glenn's brows came together. "But what do *you* want?"

I need to stay focused. Clair quickly brought her mind back to the conversation. *Let's see. Glenn asked me about the shop.* "Ima had already ordered some of the new books and gifts." She drew in a deep breath and tried to continue. "But. . ."

"Yes?"

"It's not easy for me." Clair sighed. "I have to deal with customers. Greet them. And I will need to hire some part-time help. I'm afraid I'll either say the wrong things. . .or nothing at all. . .or too much. Just like right now." She looked down at her hands, trying not to think about the look on Hudson's face.

"That's why I'm here. To make the way smoother for you. But, if you don't mind my asking, how did someone so smart and lovely as yourself decide she wasn't smart and lovely? You must have had a rough road growing up." His eyes were filled with compassion—just as they had been that night in the limousine, when he had seen her house for the first time.

Clair wondered how he could have known about her childhood. *He's very perceptive.* She decided to keep revelations of her past to a minimum. "My stepfather was a hardworking man but poor as a church mouse, as they say. I think it must have been a burden for him. . .to raise me." She twisted a chunk of her hair around her finger.

Glenn shifted in his chair. "I shouldn't have asked you such a personal question. I apologize." He cleared his throat and looked at her. "I have faith in you, Clair O'Neal. In spite of your hesitations, I think once we do some tweaking, you'll make quite the businesswoman."

"I'm wood," Clair mumbled to herself.

"What did you say?"

Clair blushed. "I'm sorry. I don't mean to be impolite. It's just that I've always been like a block of wood. . .with people." *Does Hudson see me that way, too?* "I'm not sure how I can be fixed."

"You can make a work of art out of a chunk of wood. You just need the right tools. As an image coach, I have those tools."

Change. Clair picked up her water goblet to diffuse a growing uneasiness in the pit of her stomach, but her hand shook so much she had to set it back down. She breathed a prayer and summoned all her courage. Then she looked straight into the eyes of the man who claimed he could help her conquer her fears and set her on a new path. "Well then, Mr. Yves,"—she forced her shoulders back—"how shall we begin?"

eight

Glenn seemed pleasantly surprised with her response. "Well, first you mentioned saying the wrong things to customers. You can always slow down a bit. Think about what you're going to say and then say it distinctly. There's no rush. Smile when you speak. Look directly into people's eyes when you're talking to them."

"Okay." Clair made an effort to keep her gaze from constantly darting away.

"Very good." Glenn smiled. "And during conversations, some people aren't listening. My grandmother always called these folks prairie dogs. They stay down in their holes, not paying attention. Then they pop up their little heads when it's their turn to talk. They'll usually have a surprised look on their faces, because they haven't a clue as to what was said." He raised an eyebrow. "Even though you don't always look at me, I believe you are listening. People will think you're a good conversationalist simply because you pay attention to what they're saying. And that's all I'm going to cover on listening, since I think it's your strong suit."

"It is?" Clair couldn't believe she'd impressed Glenn. She bit her lower lip, wondering why she suddenly felt so warm and prickly.

"But about that chewing on your lower lip. . . You're making little pink marks underneath your lips. So, you'll want to retrain yourself not to indulge in that habit."

Clair nodded quickly, wanting to please him. "You're right.

I'll try to stop."

"Good girl." Glenn cleared his throat. "Now, about confidence around people. Like at the party the other evening. If you're in a crowded room, the best thing to do is search for someone who looks more afraid than you do. Make it your goal to make that person feel better. . .more comfortable. Then you've helped two people at the same time. And you might even make a new friend."

"Is that what you were doing?" Clair almost bit her lip but chose to lick it instead.

"What do you mean?"

"The night of the party. You made me feel more at ease. Were you afraid of something, too?" The second the words came out, she regretted them. Every time she loosened up with people, nonsense poured out of her mouth.

"You *do* listen." Glenn shook his finger and grinned. "You want to know if I was uneasy. Well, like I said, everyone has his or her moment. That night, just before I saw you, I'd gotten off the phone with a client who'd just lost her mother to pneumonia. I saw you and thought I could cheer us both up."

"I understand."

Glenn looked at her with an earnest gaze. "Yes, I know you do."

Thunder crackled in the distance. Oddly, the sky seemed clear and the sun still shone brightly. When Clair looked back at him, she noticed something else in Glenn's expression. Something knowing—and yet searching. *What is he looking for?*

"Life is full of surprises. And sometimes, they take us by storm." He grinned.

Was he being philosophical, or should she ask him what he meant? Since she'd spent little time visiting with people, the protocol eluded her. She shivered, wishing she'd brought a sweater to the restaurant.

And she still felt that irritating pebble in her shoe. With her feet, she tried to turn her shoe over to empty it as inconspicuously as possible, but suddenly the shoe flipped away, just out of reach. Clair glanced under the table, hoping Glenn hadn't noticed.

To Clair's horror, Glenn rose from his chair and then lowered himself next to her. "I'm so sorry." She bit her lower lip.

"I see you've lost your slipper." He retrieved the stray shoe and, taking hold of her ankle, added, "Let's just see if it fits." He gingerly slipped the shoe back on her foot and smiled. "There you go."

Right away Clair thought about the run in her hose from her fall and the hole in her shoe. *How embarrassing.* But how could she ever forget his compassion? Never. She managed a bashful thank-you.

"You're very welcome." He looked up at her.

She saw that knowing smile again. *Who is this man?* And wasn't he going way beyond the duties of an image coach?

A woman with long auburn hair stepped over to their table. "Glenn, what are you doing crawling around on the floor?" she asked. "That move wasn't in your coaching manual!" Her laughter sounded almost musical—like water rolling over river rocks. Clair liked her right away.

Glenn stood and smiled as he spoke her name. "Katherine. You look lovely."

Clair had to agree. The woman's jade-colored outfit suited her in every way, and her hair and makeup added to the overall effect.

"Thank you." The woman kissed him, leaving a scarlet imprint on his cheek. She turned to Clair with a warm and inviting smile. "And who do we have here?"

Glenn seated himself. "Katherine, this is Clair O'Neal. Clair, this is Katherine Burke, a former client of mine."

"Good to meet you." Katherine extended her hand.

"I'm glad to meet you, too." Clair lifted her trembling hand, and the elegant woman gave it a warm shake. She appeared to be the very epitome of gracefulness and charm. Clearly, her time under Glenn's tutelage had paid off. Clair sighed. Oh, if only *she* could come off as polished and refined. Was such a thing really possible?

Katherine nodded in her direction and responded as if reading her thoughts. "Meeting Glenn was truly one of the best things that ever happened to me."

Glenn's eyes glistened, but a slight look of embarrassment crossed his face.

"I confess I didn't give him much to work with. . ." Katherine added with a look of chagrin. "At first, anyway."

"Of course you did," he argued. Glenn turned to Clair. "Katherine has a natural love for life—and for people. I just needed to draw that out. And she's a wonderful Christian woman, so that made our working relationship even more pleasant. We had a number of things in common. Still do."

Katherine nodded. "I always say the Lord sent Glenn to me at just the right time. My career was just taking off, and I needed a little encouragement to step out into the public eye. I was always such a shy little thing."

Shy? Clair could hardly imagine it. Why, this woman was anything but. Katherine exuded confidence. It showed in her smile. Her sparkling eyes. Her hands, which didn't appear to tremble in the slightest as she reached up with one to brush an imaginary speck of dust from her jacket.

Katherine turned as a gentleman in a tailored suit approached from behind her. "I'm sorry, but I must go now. Work awaits. . ."

"Katherine, it was a pleasure, as always." Glenn stood to his feet.

Clair couldn't help but wonder if he did this for all women as they came and went from tables.

Katherine took his hand once more. "It was wonderful seeing you again, Glenn. And I enjoyed meeting you, Clair." The refined woman nodded in their direction.

Clair returned the gesture with a smile.

As Katherine turned on her heel, thunder rolled outside and then swelled into a deep booming rumble that rattled the window by their table.

"She always did like a sensational exit," Glenn said with a laugh as he took his seat once again.

Clair couldn't help but sigh. "She seems so. . .ideal."

He laughed. "She's come a long way from the nervous, withdrawn girl I used to know." He paused for a moment then looked Clair in the eye. "I can polish the outside," he explained, "but sincerity and kindness come from the inside. It's already a part of you, Clair. That's something of the heart. Something of *real* value. And something I can never teach."

Before Clair could stop herself, she reached out and touched Glenn's hand. Then, with a fingertip, she pointed at his cheek to remind him of the lipstick imprint Katherine had left behind. He chuckled and wiped it away.

The waiter made an appearance with their salads and a loaf of hot bread.

"Looks good." Glenn said. "Thanks, Ty."

Clair stared back and forth from her food to her flatware, sighing at the sticky situation before her. Which fork should she use for the salad? She never could seem to remember.

Glenn picked up the smaller fork and stuck it into some salad leaves.

She followed his lead and began to munch on her spinach salad, which was garnished with walnuts, mandarin oranges, and a delicate dressing. She ate slowly, letting the flavors linger on her tongue as she listened carefully to Glenn's speech on confidence and poise.

Clair asked questions, and he answered them patiently. Finally, he mentioned other essentials, such as hair, makeup, and dress. She could feel herself wanting to bite her lip, but she straightened her shoulders instead. *How can I tell him I have no money for such indulgences?* "I don't have the—"

"Please." Glenn raised his hand. "I already know what you're trying to say. But when I made this offer to you, I immediately made an appointment for you at Armando's Spa and Boutique. The services have already been paid for."

"Oh, but I can't. I couldn't expect—"

"I insist. There's no reason to tell an angel how beautiful she is without giving her the wings to fly." Glenn lit up with another smile.

Clair's thoughts flew, at once, to Katherine Burke. The beautiful woman had taken Glenn's teaching to heart and the payoff was obvious. If Clair went along with his plan, would she one day have Katherine's confidence and grace?

On the other hand, was accepting such a generous gift from someone she barely knew appropriate? Would there be unsuitable expectations? She almost laughed at the thought. No one could possibly be interested in her in an amorous way. She wasn't the sort to date, and men seemed to pick up on that. Didn't they?

"Walter Sullivan did the same for me," Glenn went on to say. "He even paid to have my teeth straightened. I certainly wasn't born with these pearlies."

"Do you mind if I ask why he did so much?"

"Because he'd been very successful, and he wanted to do something that had nothing to do with making more money. He was a rare individual and one of the people in my life whom I truly respected."

Clair nodded at Glenn and decided to take one final look over at Hudson's table. Amazingly, the woman with him was still talking, and Hudson was still listening. His shoulders sagged as badly as her living room couch.

Should she be happy about that? *Oh dear. Has Glenn said something, and I wasn't listening again?* Clair placed her hand over her mouth in dismay. "What did you say? I am so sorry."

"What's the matter?" He reached his hand out to her.

Clair blushed. "I've been such a prairie dog."

Glenn threw his head back in laughter.

&

After eating more luscious food than Clair had ever eaten in her life and after listening to more suggestions and advice than she'd ever thought existed, she was deposited back at her shop with a very agreeable good-bye. She waved and then watched until Glenn disappeared down the street.

Suddenly the appointment he'd made for her at Armando's Spa and Boutique came to mind. She'd certainly keep the appointment, but not without some anxiety. What would the technicians think of her? Would they feel she was a dusty moth trying to be a butterfly? There'd be rooms full of pretty women, all perfumed and groomed, and there'd she be—Miss Ragamuffin, the name her stepfather had always called her.

Wiping the straggly hairs from her face, she reached over to the light switch. *But if I am to run this bookstore, I don't want to look shabby.* She glanced around at the boxes, which had arrived just prior to Ima's death. They contained the latest in Bibles, books, gifts, and CDs. She sighed as she realized they would all have to be unpacked and shelved—without Ima's assistance. Clair knew the basics of running a small bookstore, of course, but the whole expansion process seemed overwhelming. Ima had wanted to change the name of the store, but she'd never told her what it would be.

There was so much to think about—so much to plan. She'd need to redo the sign outside, order new floor displays, restock the shelves, and so forth. And then there was publicity and the hiring of part-time help. *Oh my.*

Clair felt the rumbling ache of defiance within her stomach. Even though eating expensive food had been delightful, she wasn't accustomed to ingesting rich sauces and desserts. Her stomach felt as if there were some kind of skirmish going on inside. She just hoped she could keep the food down. She sat on a stool near the cash register, rubbing her stomach and missing her employer—the woman who'd been her only friend.

She noticed a slip of paper Ima had posted on the bulletin board. The note reminded her to "walk in joy and eat more soy." *Dear, sweet, funny Ima. If only I'd arrived at the shop earlier that morning, Ima might have survived.* She could have called for help at the first sign of trouble. *How can I possibly deserve this shop?*

She sighed, recalling the reading of the will. Afterward, Ima's sister, LaVerne, had insisted Clair take the business, wanting to honor her sister's request. What a dilemma. Mist filled her eyes. *No tears, Clair. No tears.*

Some of Ima's words came back to her. "If you don't have a plan, then plan for a headache." Clair smiled at the remembrance and thought how sad it would be to let Ima's dream die. But Clair could live the dream for her.

She would need to get organized. Clair rummaged around

in a top drawer behind the counter and found a large pad of paper for scribbling down notes. Preparing for a grand reopening would require a lot of work, but hard work had never been a problem.

And money? Hmm. There was still enough cash in the business account to make the switch. But what about dealing with the public? A recluse would now be forced into the "people business." Clair shook her head at the virtual impossibility of the notion. Glenn wasn't around, so she treated herself to a good lip-chewing session. Then his words came to mind. "Once we do some tweaking, you'll make quite the businesswoman." *How can he have more confidence in me than I do?*

Clair started to hum one of her favorite hymns, and soon ideas for the new store began to flow. She took copious notes on every aspect of the reopening. She stayed so busy in fact, she thought of Hudson only every fifteen minutes.

The bell over the front door jangled.

Hudson stood in the doorway clutching two cups and looking striking in his sapphire-colored shirt and denims. Steam rose from the two cups in soft, friendly curls. "How about some coffee?"

He came back. He really came back! Clair's tummy ache vanished.

nine

Hudson loved the way Clair smiled. *I think she's happy to see me.*

Clair rose from her chair, straightened her shoulders, and looked him straight in the eye. "Yes. I'd like some."

He walked over to hand her a cup. "You look different. Good, I mean." His voice had the tiniest stutter. *Oh brother.* He could sing on live television, face huge crowds, but he couldn't give Clair the simplest compliment. She did look slightly different, though—more self-assured or rested or something. Why didn't *she* seem nervous? *And why won't my lips work? It's like having a big wad of peanut butter in my mouth.*

"Thank you." Clair took a sip of her coffee. "It's good."

"You're welcome." Okay. What to say now. "I should have made a list."

"What kind of list?"

Hudson chuckled. "Sorry. You caught me mumbling out loud again." He balled up his hand. "I might as well cough it up. I wanted to talk to you about some things, but I lost them in my head." He felt the calluses on the ends of his fingers from playing the guitar, and it reminded him that all things worthwhile required work.

"I feel that way all the time," Clair said.

"You do?" He took a mouthful of his drink. *Mmm. Maybe hot caffeine will come to my rescue.* Hudson beat his brain until he thought of a subject. "How was Ima's funeral?"

Clair paused, looking lost in thought. She finally said, "It

61

was joyful because of where Ima is, but sad because I miss her so much."

"I wish. . .I'd gone." Hudson shuffled his feet, guzzled some more brew, and set the cup on the counter. "Sorry, I'm not usually this tense."

"And *I'm* not usually this relaxed." Clair's hand went to her mouth.

For some reason, she appeared astonished at what she'd just said. Hudson thought she looked cute. They both stared at each other and then chuckled.

"I'm glad you feel that way around me. It's probably good for me to flub up once in a while. Keeps me humble." He grinned. "Otherwise my sister tells me I get too self-absorbed."

"I can't imagine that." Clair offered him a stool. "Would you like to sit down?"

Hudson felt restless. "No thanks." His mind refused to let go of one fact—they'd both been dining with someone else at the same restaurant. The very day he'd chosen to ask Clair out. *Not the best turn of events.* He decided to turn his focus to the half-empty shelves. "What will happen to the shop now?"

She licked her lips. "Ima gave me the bookshop. . .in her will."

"Really?" Hudson marveled at the news. He'd never heard of an employee receiving such a generous gift. "She must have loved you like a daughter."

"She never said so, but I knew it in the things she did. She was a very precious woman." Clair took a slow sip from her cup. "Ima was going to expand the shop, adding a larger area for music and gifts. That's why the inventory on the shelves is so low right now, to make room for the changes."

"So, you're going to follow through with her plan?"

"Yes."

"It's a good idea. I think it'll do well here." Hudson wondered why she'd answered so briefly and why her voice sounded like all the air had gone out.

Clair set her cup down as her face lit up. "I don't have a name for the new store. Any ideas?"

"Let's see. . ." Hudson looked upward as he did a little brainstorming in his head. "Hmm. Okay, maybe. Nah. Don't think so. Let's see. . .heaven, harps, angels, river, gold. . ." He picked up his coffee to give his hands something to twiddle with. He was so used to creating while holding his guitar, he felt awkward without his companion to help him think. "I don't know. How about something like Rivers of Gold Christian Bookshop?"

Clair's eyes widened. "I like it very much. How did you think of it?"

"I'm not sure." He smiled. "But I'm glad you like it."

"Ima would approve." She made some notes on a pad of paper. "Thank you."

You are so welcome. "Do you need any more help?"

"I might later."

"If you ever need me, I'm right down the street. Well, you know that." Hudson stuffed his hands into the pockets of his jeans. He considered Clair's expression. *Does she wonder who I was with at the River Grill? Maybe I should tell her straight out—that the woman won a lunch with me in a charity auction. And what's the deal with Glenn Yves? Is Clair dating him?* He had no idea how to bring up a topic as prickly as cacti, but maybe he could just hover over the subject. "I was surprised to see you at the River Grill today. I've never seen you there before."

"I've never been there before."

"Well, that must be why. . .I've never seen you there before." *I'm just going in circles here. Maybe I'd better just cut to the chase.* "I'm playing at the Silver Moon Café tomorrow evening. It's a restaurant, and they have performers who. . .perform." *Oh brother.* "Would you like to go with me?"

"Yes." Clair's hand flew up to her mouth. "Yes, I would. Yes."

"All righty then." Hudson smiled, feeling confident she really wanted to go with him. Suddenly he was in the mood for his coffee again. Lots of coffee. He reached for his beverage as his enthusiasm radiated through his fingers, causing a squeezing action on his grip. He couldn't stop the gush as he watched the coffee make a slow-motion kind of rise and fall all over his very favorite shirt.

ten

Saturday morning, Clair rose early to ready herself for her big day at Armando's Spa. She scrubbed herself extra clean in the shower and dressed in some of her best clothes—a brown pantsuit from a local garage sale.

After fiddling with her hair for an hour in an effort to make it look fashionable, she gave up, letting the strands droop around her shoulders. *Oh well. I guess they can't shoot me for being ugly.* A little giggle escaped her lips, making her face light up. *I don't look quite so dull when I smile.*

When she'd primped as much as she knew how, Clair locked her front door and headed down the sidewalk. Since she still couldn't afford to fix her car, she left the house early so she'd have time for the twelve-block hike to Armando's.

After a breeze had whipped her hair to shreds, and her feet throbbed in her too-small shoes, she spotted the spa across the street. Her anxiety swelled as she dipped from the pot of fears that'd been accumulating since Glenn had told her about the makeover.

Every part of Clair wanted to turn around and walk back home, but Glenn had been so generous, she couldn't disappoint him. *And maybe I should make the most of the gift since tonight is my very first date.* At that moment, Clair let something seep into her life—anticipation. A foreign word to her trembling heart. *Hudson.* She'd be on a real date and one she'd cherish forever. *I guess Hudson really wasn't dating that woman at the River Grill.*

Clair gathered up some gumption and marched over to the spa like a woman on a mission. She paused at the big double doors in front, which were painted a cobalt blue and lacquered to a mirror finish, then bit down hard on her lower lip and reached for the handle. *Maybe a smile would help.*

The moment she entered the posh surroundings of Armando's, a woman in an elegant white dress and with silver hair, glided toward her as if she were floating on a hovercraft. "Oh, *soyez le bienvenu*! Welcome! You must be Clair."

Clair nodded briskly. "Hi." The sounds of falling water and classical music flowed around her.

"Well, *mademoiselle*, I'm Destinee Armando, and we've been waiting for you." The woman stared at Clair, looking at both sides of her profile. "Hmm. Mr. Yves was correct. You have fabulous bone structure. Oh, we have lots to work with. But such tragic eyes."

Clair just listened, not really knowing what to say. Did she really look tragic? She brightened her smile.

"Mr. Yves has taken care of everything. You are just here to enjoy the delights." Her hands swept upward, her long, manicured nails highlighted by the gesture. "Are we ready?"

"Yes." She tried not to stare at Destinee, who was unquestionably beautiful with her flawless makeup, chic hairstyle, and impeccable clothes. Clair felt so out of her league, the urge to hide became overwhelming. She spotted a closet door, and it looked tempting. *Come on now. You're being silly.*

Destinee led her into a small room full of pastel-colored lockers. "You may undress in here and then slip on one of those fluffy robes. Would you like champagne or sparkling water?"

Clair folded her hands in front of her. "Water, please."

"Very well. Come out when you are ready." Then like a

petal on a stream, she drifted off.

Clair slipped out of her clothes and into the lush blue robe. She opened the door and peeked out. *Am I supposed to wait here?* Trying to shed some of her shyness, she crept out into the main room. She could get a better look at the décor now. *Oh my.* A quaint Italian motif with a cascading fountain in the middle—she'd never seen anything like it.

Suddenly, a group of women, in various stages of beautification, swooped through like a flock of blue herons. She pulled herself out of their way as she tightened her robe. No one even noticed her.

Just when Clair thought about scurrying back to the locker room, Destinee appeared out of nowhere. She handed Clair a crystal goblet of sparkling water with a slice of lime and then escorted her through a hallway and into a small room lit only by candles. A massage bed sat in the middle of the room. Piano music and the scent of lavender drifted through the air. The familiar psalm ran through Clair's head once again. *He makes me lie down in green pastures.* What a delicious present this day was turning out to be.

Then something—or rather, *someone*—caught her eye. A buxom woman with broad shoulders and muscular arms stood before her like a Viking. All she lacked was the helmet with horns.

The bulky woman slapped her enormous hands together. "*Gut.*"

The sight tickled Clair's funny bone. *Is this comical?* Her sense of humor had been sequestered for so many years, she wasn't certain.

"This is Helga, your massage therapist," Destinee said. "By the time she's done with you, you'll be so relaxed, your bones won't even feel attached to your body!"

Clair swallowed hard.

"*Fraulein,*" Helga said, smacking the massage table. "Are ve ready?"

Destinee lifted the glass of water out of Clair's suspended hand and then left the room, doing that floating thing again.

Twenty minutes later, after Clair had been rubbed, pounded, and kneaded like bread dough, she started to unwind a little.

"Gut," Helga barked.

By now Clair realized the woman merely sounded gruff. In fact, Helga seemed determined to make sure she'd be pleased with the results. Clair almost laughed at herself for being so anxious over such a simple thing as a massage, but she'd grown up with so little physical contact, the sensations felt peculiar to her. After a while though, Clair started to enjoy herself.

What would Ima think if she could see her now? She'd probably say, "Make the most of it, kid. It's supposed to be fun!"

Thirty minutes later, Helga removed the cucumber pads from Clair's eyes and directed her to another room on the other side of the facility. Clair was so relaxed she could barely walk. Still, she could hardly wait to see what exciting adventures lay ahead.

Next on the day's agenda were a body polish, an herbal wrap, and a European facial. Then on to the hair designer for a haircut, subtle highlights, and a deep condition. In between all the pamperings, the attendants offered Clair sumptuous goodies. As she tasted the orchid tea and the scones, she tried to memorize every flavor and every sensation of the day, since she knew such luxuries would never come again.

After lunch, Clair had both a manicure and a pedicure, which included massages with peppermint balm and dips in warm paraffin. Then a new batch of technicians took over, reshaping her heavy eyebrows and giving her a rather laborious application of makeup. When they were finished, the staff gave her several gifts bags of makeup and hair care products to take home. Clair's mind staggered with the idea that Glenn had paid for such extravagances.

Just when Clair thought everyone had finished, someone escorted her into the adjoining boutique with the promise of finding the perfect outfits to enhance her coloring and figure. She'd never considered such a concept before, since the only things she'd ever purchased were garage sale items and leftovers on clearance tables. Still, before all was said and done, she had selected nearly a dozen new ensembles to hang in her closet. Oh, how drab those old clothes would look now draped alongside these new, fashionable ones.

When Clair's day at the spa was finally complete and she'd been dressed in blue silk finery, Destinee led her to a full-length gilded mirror.

Clair saw herself and stepped back. Then slowly, she leaned in closer. *Could this really be me?* She touched her face and hair and new silky dress.

"Well, mademoiselle, what do you think?" Destinee placed her hands on her hips and raised her chin. "You are the masterpiece, and we are the artists. We are *très bon*. No?"

Out of the blue, the employees as well as the other clients broke into applause. Even stoic Helga seemed misty-eyed as she looked at her and hollered, "*Schon.*" Clair assumed that was something good.

Feeling a little embarrassed with the sudden attention, Clair wanted to hide or at least twirl her finger in her hair, but with a prayer and some grit, she let go of her timidity and grinned with excitement. The day had turned out light years beyond anything she'd imagined. "I don't know what to say." She felt herself choking up as she tried to express her gratitude. *My cup overflows.* "I think all of you are. . .*magnifique!*" *Where in the world did that come from? I guess the mouse has finally squeaked!*

Destinee nodded, looking pleased with her response. In the midst of another agreeable uproar, a male figure emerged from the patrons and staff. Glenn stood a few yards away, sporting a tweed jacket and a generous smile. He was like her fairy godfather suddenly appearing to make sure the magic had worked. It had. Clair's fingers reached up to her lips to keep her emotions in check. *No tears, Clair. This is a happy time.*

Glenn took a few steps toward her, his gaze never leaving her. She felt a rush of gratitude and wanted to thank him with a kiss but stopped herself since she thought it might be improper.

"Miss Clair O'Neal. . .you look drop-dead gorgeous." Glenn raised an eyebrow.

A sigh rippled through the crowd. Destinee nodded, and Helga clapped her hands.

Clair could feel herself flushing a deep crimson, but she didn't mind this time, since the words and the moment had brought so much pleasure to Glenn. But as she boldly gazed into his eyes, something else lingered in his expression— something new to her. *Could it be attraction? For me?* She dismissed the musings as she straightened her shoulders, gathered her hands to her heart, and mouthed the words, "Thank you so much."

eleven

Hudson knocked on Clair's front door for the second time. Had he written down the right address? A truck rumbled by, leaving a wake of noise and blue smoke. *Maybe Clair changed her mind.*

No, thankfully the door opened, and a woman who looked like Clair emerged from the house. "Clair?" He tried not to stare, but he felt utterly helpless not to. The woman had the same soft brown eyes like a doe and delicate smile as Clair, but something had happened to the rest of her. Her hair, clothes, and well, everything else about her looked transformed. She'd been a lovely woman before, but now she appeared dazzling in her blue dress. *I'm staring like an ape. Okay, I'm going to look at the ground now.*

"Hi," Clair said.

Good, same voice. "You look. . .*radiant.*" Hudson wondered if he should ask her what happened or if that would be rude.

Clair put her hand over her mouth, looking a little worried. "I went to a spa."

"Well, you sure got your money's worth." *Oh brother. I'm sounding like a country bumpkin now.* "You look incredible. I mean, well, you always looked pretty." *Oh man.* "But now, even more so."

A shining smile lit up her countenance. "Thank you."

"Are you ready?" He looked at her elegant attire and then at his jeans and black shirt. Maybe he should have dressed up a little more.

Clair locked her door and rushed down the path ahead of him. *Why is she in such a hurry to get away?* Was she self-conscious

71

about her house? It didn't matter a bit to him where she lived. Hudson caught up with her, and with his hand gently against her back, ushered her to his pickup. Once he had her safely tucked inside, he trotted around to the driver's side, relieved his vehicle was clean for a change.

Once they'd arrived at the Silver Moon Café, Hudson got Clair settled in his favorite spot, walked up the stairs to the stage, and waited for Big George Cummings, the owner, to introduce him. He looked around, still trying to absorb the newly renovated interior of the café—brick walls, black ceiling, and a larger stage area. *Nice.*

Big George appeared from the other side of the stage, grabbed the microphone, and gave his usual animated spiel like a grizzly bear on espresso.

While the audience applauded, Hudson strode toward the spotlight. He lifted his guitar from its stand and made himself comfortable on a stool. He gazed out over the audience and offered a grin, then cleared this throat. "Good evening. I'm Hudson Mandel."

The crowd applauded again, and he glanced down at Clair. He felt another tug. Would she think him too forward to sing the song he'd written for her? *Is it too soon?*

When the inspiration hit, he'd barely been able to write the words down fast enough. They'd come from a place in his heart that had never been touched before.

A baby let out a squall in the back, reminding him he was on stage, so he turned his attention to his music.

"I wrote this song for someone special. I call it 'Clair.' Hope you like it." Hudson started to pick out his tune while singing along. When he came to the chorus, he sang:

"Ever since I saw your face

I have never been the same,

I lose a piece of my heart
Every time I say your name."

When Hudson wrapped up his song, a startling silence permeated the room, and then the stillness was replaced with booming applause. He'd avoided Clair's eyes during the song, but he couldn't wait any longer to see her reaction, so he gazed down at her. She appeared as luminous as she looked confused. *I'll take that as encouragement.*

Hudson played a few more tunes and then decided to take a short break. He walked up to Clair's table and slid into the chair next to her. The glow from the incandescent light above created a halo effect around her head.

"The audience loved you," she said.

"But did *you* love me?"

"Yes." She clasped her hands together, smiling. "Very much."

He knew Clair's words referred to only his performance, but he wondered if she could ever feel more.

"Your folk songs are rich and original and affecting." She drew back as if surprised by her own words and then she touched his hand. "I *love* your music."

Clair obviously had no idea of the impact of her compliments or of the soft touch of her hand. Hudson wanted to kiss her mouth this minute, but he would be a patient man. "You're my favorite critic so far."

Clair laughed.

She seemed wonderfully different. Still Clair, but more open with her thoughts. He couldn't fathom the psyche of a woman, but he wondered if the trip to the spa had given her more confidence. Or perhaps she simply felt more comfortable being around him. Whatever it was, he liked it. "I hope you didn't mind. . .about the song."

"Mind?"

"The song, 'Clair.' I wrote it. . .you know. . .for you." Why did he get so tongue-tied around her?

"I wasn't sure." She fiddled with her napkin. "I didn't want to presume."

"You're the only Clair I know."

"Thank you." Her head dipped down. "I feel honored." When she looked up, her eyes were misty.

"You're welcome." Hudson gave her hand a squeeze. "Are you hungry? Maybe we should order something before I go back on stage." He gave a signal to one of the waiters.

Otto, a portly man who dropped more plates than a Greek dancer, barreled over to them. "Here we are," he said as he handed them their menus. When Otto saw Clair, his jowls shimmied a bit. Then after he took their beverage requests, he stood transfixed, gaping at her.

"Otto." Hudson cleared his throat to release the poor man from his trance. "Thank you."

"Sorry." Otto shrugged his shoulders and grinned. "I'll be back in a minute with your drinks."

Clair didn't even seem to notice Otto's ogling. In fact, when she looked up from the menu, she had a faraway gaze. Hudson leaned toward her. "I would love to know what you're thinking."

"Actually. . .today is my birthday." She licked her lips. "And your song was by far the finest present I've ever gotten."

"Thank you. But really, *today* is your birthday?"

She brightened. "I'm thirty-one years old."

"We're the same age." Hudson grinned.

"Really?"

"How did you overlook your birthday? Didn't the cards from relatives and friends tip you off?"

"My relatives are all gone." Clair set her menu down and sighed. "And Ima was my only real friend." She chuckled. "It sounds so Charles Dickens-ish when I say it out loud."

Hudson reached to touch her hand, at once feeling her pain. He hadn't known the extent of Clair's solitude. He wanted to know more but didn't want to come off too pushy.

Before he could think of a comment, Otto arrived, this time a little more restrained. He brought their drinks, took their orders, and then shambled off toward the kitchen.

Hudson looked back at Clair. "So, what did your parents do for your birthday when you were little?"

"I never knew my father, and my mother died when I was very young." Clair's shoulders slumped. "And my stepfather... well...he saw no need to celebrate birthdays."

Hudson saw the sadness in her eyes. His heart went out to Clair—to the little girl who'd been ignored growing up. He couldn't imagine such behavior in his family, since his birthday, as well as his sister's, had always been a colossal affair. He hesitated inquiring further into her past, but he had to put his mind at ease with one more question. "Your stepfather...did he treat you well otherwise?"

"He was never the same after my mother passed away." Clair folded her arms around her middle. "He didn't like to spend time with me, even when he had the opportunity. I always got the feeling he felt he'd been stuck with me. I guess he just didn't know what to do with a daughter."

Hudson drew in a deep breath and held his tongue.

"I had my own way of coping." Clair's gaze shifted downward. "I worked hard around the house—did my chores, kept things clean. I guess I thought he would notice me that way, but after a while I just felt kind of invisible...at least to him. And I always felt like that at school, too. I wasn't what you would call a social child. Never really found a group to fit in with."

Hudson found it hard to believe anyone could overlook Clair but didn't interrupt her story.

"I got it in my mind that people didn't like to be around me," she continued, "especially my stepfather, so I steered clear of him. There was a little room up in the attic. . .my mother had used it for storage. Some of her things were still there after she died. It might seem strange, but I felt close to her when I went into that space. I guess I just started using it as a sanctuary, of sorts."

"Understandable." *But horribly sad.*

Clair's eyes filled with tears. "I have to admit, half the time I'd go up those stairs to get away from my stepfather, and half the time I sat up there, wishing he would call out to me, ask me to come down and watch TV or play a game with him." She used her fingertip to brush the moisture from her lashes. "Sorry. It's still a little hard to talk about."

Hudson gathered Clair's hands into his. "I'm sorry."

Clair paused for a minute as if she were collecting her thoughts. "Sometimes I would sit up there till evening, just to see if he would notice I was missing. I'd rummage through the boxes of my mother's things and imagine what life would have been like, if she'd lived. I'd dress up in her clothes and pretend to be beautiful."

You are beautiful.

"As the light shifted in the room I imagined monsters in the shadows." She smiled. "I think all kids do that, even in their bedrooms. But I had no one to run to when I got scared. No one to hold me."

I would have held you.

She tilted her head, looking as withdrawn as she had the

first day he'd met her. With all the clinking and chattering around them, he suddenly wished they were in a more private place. "You don't have to talk about this, if you don't want to." Hudson squeezed her hand as he wondered what kind of a man would neglect a child in such a way.

"It's okay." She took a slow sip of her root beer. "I wasn't afraid. Just lonesome. I spent a lot of time looking out the window. I think I grew up watching life more than living it. But I learned how to entertain myself. . .by singing." Her eyes lit up a little. "It's amazing what a child can do, when left to her own devices. Music became very important to me during my alone time. I think it was God's way of ministering to me—and me, to Him."

"So, that little room became a prayer closet, of sorts?" he asked.

She shrugged. "I wouldn't have known to call it that then, though I certainly sensed God's presence in there." Her eyes brightened. "And I don't want to make it sound like I had no interaction with other children. I made a couple of friends over the years, and there was this one little boy. . .one summer. He somehow managed to rig a pulley from his tree house over to my window. And he sent me little bunches of flowers and funny notes." Clair's hand went to her cheek. "We never met in person, and he didn't sign his name, so I never knew who he was, or. . ." Her voice faded. "In one of his notes, he said he loved me, that he was coming back to rescue me someday."

"I wish that boy had been me."

A forlorn look came over her. "He and his family moved away at the end of the same summer, but I kept all of his little notes. In fact, I took special care of the last one. It's buried in a box, somewhere among my mother's things in the attic. I never saw the boy again, but I've always remembered his kindness. It brought some light during a dark time. . .like a bright warm sun coming up just for me." Suddenly, she looked embarrassed. "I'm sorry. I didn't mean to go on and on about myself."

"No, it's fine." Hudson gazed into her eyes, wishing she were in his arms. "It's your day, after all." He sighed. "If only I'd known the secret to your heart, I would've written you a letter, too." He gave her a wink. "Especially on a day like today."

Clair's cheeks glowed pink.

Without warning, Otto exploded over to their table, interrupting the perfect moment. But to Otto's credit, he lowered the heaping plates in front of them without a single mishap. When two of the other waiters applauded at his flawless service, Otto rolled his eyes. "Where's the faith?"

Hudson turned around to discover Tara Williamson rushing his way.

"Where in the world have you been?" Tara gave Hudson a possessive hug and a kiss on the cheek. "I haven't seen you in ages." Her voice had a flirtatious edge to it. "By the way, Hudson, you look fantastic in black. I think you forgot just how great. . .that color can be." She tucked a long, dark curl behind her ear.

"Thanks." Hudson flinched a bit as he took note of her slinky black dress then turned to Clair. "I'd like you to meet Tara Williamson. Tara, this is Clair O'Neal."

Tara made a fist with her hand and held it to her stomach. "Of course, the song, 'Clair.' It was for you."

"I'm glad to meet you." Clair held her hand out to Tara.

"Same here." Instead of shaking her hand, Tara waved to her parents.

Stanley and Joan Williamson rushed over, dressed to the

hilt and gushing all the way. After the introductions, the attention turned back to Hudson.

"Well, Maestro," Stanley said. "Your performance gets better every time we hear you."

"You were wonderful, dear." Joan straightened Hudson's collar. "By the way, when are you coming over for dinner again? We miss you. *Tara* misses you."

"Mother, really." Tara shook her head but looked intently at Hudson.

"Thanks for the invitation." Hudson groaned inside, thinking Joan's comment sounded like a sour note in an otherwise harmonious evening. He glanced at Clair, hoping she hadn't heard the remark, but he couldn't quite read her expression.

"Well, don't make yourself so scarce," Stanley said to Hudson. "And I hope you've had some time to think about my offer. It's still good." He slapped Hudson on the back.

"Sometime we want to show you the photos from the trip we all took to Switzerland." Joan patted Hudson's arm. "Okay?"

"I might drop by sometime," Hudson said, trying to be polite. "Thanks."

"Well, good to see you, son." Stanley looked over at Clair. "And nice to meet you, Blair."

"Her name is *Clair*, Daddy. Hudson wrote a song for her. Remember?"

"Oh yes. Sorry, Clair." Stanley smacked his hands together. "We'd better get rolling. We're headed to some chick flick, which I love as much as heartburn, but the women outvoted me." He winked.

After a gush of good-byes and an exit by the Williamson family, Hudson sat back down. He could see the bemused smile on Clair's face. "I'm sorry about that. They mean well.

But they've got me all wrong. You see, they've always wanted me to marry their daughter. They're always scheming, which is why he mentioned an offer. They have this plan. I'll marry Tara, we'll sing together, and we'll live happily ever after."

"Oh?" Clair chewed on her lower lip. "Is it a plan you'd consider?"

"No." Hudson hoped to make himself very clear. "I will *never* marry Tara."

"Okay." Clair met his eyes. "Do you mind if I ask. . .what the offer was?" She folded her hands in her lap. "I'm sorry. I shouldn't have asked."

"I will tell you." Hudson covered her hands with his. "Stanley has more money than he knows what to do with. So, he's always said if I marry Tara, he'll buy the Silver Moon Café and give it to me as a wedding present. But I could never accept his offer. It's ridiculous. I don't love her. I've always liked Tara and her parents. They treat me like family. But you can't be forced to love someone, even if it appears to be a good idea for everyone involved. It's too medieval to think that way. It's not the nature of love."

"I don't know much about love." Clair's shoulders relaxed. "But I think it might feel a little like flannel pj's."

"That's right. Like a warm, soft. . .embrace." He leaned over, wanting to kiss her cheek before he headed up on stage, but out of the corner of his eye, he noticed yet another person coming toward their table. Next time, he would have to remember to take Clair on a date away from the crowd, a place where they could sit and talk quietly—just the two of them.

Clair's expression lit up as Glenn Yves approached.

Great. Hudson took a good look at the fellow. Sure, he was tall, wore an Italian suit. And yes, Glenn was probably considered handsome by some females, but why did he look at Clair as if he had some claim on her? Hudson tried not to narrow his eyes, but he certainly wanted to. "Glenn, how are you?"

"Great." Glenn smiled as he gazed at Clair. "I just wanted to say hello to Clair. Hope you don't mind."

After handshakes and small talk, Hudson was glad to see Glenn move on. He glanced at his watch. His break was over, so he took a couple of bites of his sirloin steak soup then stood to make his way back toward the stage.

"You hardly touched your food," Clair noted.

"Doesn't matter. I'll be up on stage gazing down at you. Plenty of sustenance. . .like a seven-course meal."

He watched a warm smile spread across her face—a smile he could bask in for a lifetime. *God help me. My heart is no longer mine. How did this happen?* He gave her a wink and strode up to the stage.

As he glanced back, he noticed Glenn stationing himself at a table near Clair. In spite of his rising annoyance, there wasn't much he could do about it. He'd have to put his relationship with Clair in God's hands, even though it wouldn't be easy. He certainly couldn't force her to fall in love with him any more than the Williamsons could force him to marry Tara.

After the spotlight illuminated Hudson, he said into the microphone, "I've always loved living here in Little Rock. . . the city by the river."

A few people let out a whoop of approval, making Hudson grin. "This is a little song I wrote while sailing down the Arkansas River. I hope you feel the same way." He began his song and strummed his way to the chorus. This time he gazed into Clair's lovely eyes as he sang:

"Whenever I lose myself
The river can find me.

Whenever my life is bound,
The river sets me free."

Just as Hudson wound up his tune, he noticed Clair's gaze shift to Glenn, who leaned in toward her. *What is he up to?*

Glenn began to chat with her intimately—like two-peas-in-a-pod intimately. A few seconds later, he was laughing at something she'd said.

Clair suddenly knocked over her glass of water, and Otto, who hadn't broken a plate all evening, came to her rescue, knocking over two trays of food in the process.

Glenn got up, but Otto continued his comedy of errors by inadvertently hitting him with his elbow. Glenn stepped backward, losing his footing, and took quite a tumble to the floor, with his feet actually rising above his head like in a cartoon.

Hudson wasn't a genius when it came to the subtleties of love, but he knew one thing for certain—he wasn't the only one falling head over heels for Clair.

twelve

Later, after Hudson brought her home, Clair closed her front door, scolding herself for the fiasco at the café. What in the world had gone wrong? Why was she so clumsy and silly?

In spite of her ongoing censures, Clair readied herself for bed and gave herself the luxury of bringing up a few of the brighter moments of the evening. In particular, the way Hudson sang to her, and then later brought a cake out from the kitchen to celebrate her birthday. His gaze had been full of tenderness and affection.

And then there was the way Glenn seemed to hang on her every word. Hudson may have been perturbed with Glenn's presence, but she couldn't be sure. Perhaps these were merely the pathetic imaginings of a desperate woman. *God, even if there is more to their feelings, do I deserve their attentions? Both Hudson and Glenn belong to "the beautifuls." Who am I?* A question she'd been trying to answer her whole life.

She slipped on her old nightgown, the one she'd worn so much it had become like velvet against her skin. Ima—and her sweet ways—came to mind. *She used to call me* beloved. And hadn't Hudson used that very word in his song about her?

Clair gazed in the mirror, studying herself. "You are beloved," she whispered and smiled. *Hmm. It sounds unfamiliar, but welcome. Very welcome.*

After scooting underneath the covers, she let go of all the bittersweetness of the evening and began to sail away into a deep sleep.

Many hours later, she woke up to the sound of her alarm clock. She yawned and stretched, knowing she should get out of bed but wanting to linger a few minutes before dressing for church.

Clair spent a few blissful moments coming awake then reached for her Bible. As was so often the case, she turned to the book of Psalms, reading aloud the verse that gave her the courage to face this season of her life. " 'The Lord is my shepherd, I shall not be in want. He makes me lie down in green pastures, he leads me beside quiet waters.' "

Her thoughts shifted to the banks of the Arkansas River. She closed her eyes and pictured the Lord taking her by the hand and leading her to the very edge of the water, to sit in peaceful solitude and enjoy the view. Her heart swelled at the thought of it. God—the Maker of the Universe—wanted to spend time with her. To draw her to a quiet, intimate place. To call her His *beloved*, just as Ima had done. To wash away the pain from the past in the mighty rivers of His love.

"God, my Father. . ." She started to whisper a prayer but stumbled across the word *Father*. Visions of her stepfather came to mind right away, but she pressed them back and forged ahead. Clair poured out her heart to the Lord, thanking Him for all of the marvelous changes in her life over the past several days. She prayed for His guidance regarding the bookstore, and for His will concerning her new friendships.

Afterward, she felt the strangest sensation—as if the Lord had swept into the room and lifted her into His arms. For the first time in a long while, she truly felt as if she could conquer all of the demons of the past. She pondered these things as she showered and dressed for church. And she continued to think about them as she went into the kitchen to grab a bite to eat before heading out.

Her reflections were interrupted by a rap on the front door. Clair set down her muffin and hurried toward the door. Through the peephole, she could see an elderly woman dressed in raggedy clothes. Clair opened the door. "Yes?"

"I'm Harriet Plow. You the O'Neal girl?" The woman clutched an enormous handbag, which looked like hunks of faded tapestry sewn together to make a satchel.

"Yes, I am."

"Used to live next door to you. Right over there." She pointed her bony finger to the tan house with green shutters. "Glad I found you. Thought you'd be gone by now—moved on from this forsaken place." The woman released a wheezing kind of chortle.

As Clair considered Mrs. Plow's features and voice, memories trickled back. "Yeah, I do remember." Clair opened the door wider. "I could make tea."

"Won't trouble you for any fancy drinks. But I could sure use a place to take a load off. My dogs are howling."

Clair led the woman through the door, noticing she hadn't had a bath in ages. *I wonder why she's here.* Perhaps she needed some kind of help. The older woman eased herself down on an armchair while Clair sat across from her.

"You grew up to be a real beauty." Mrs. Plow's sharp black eyes seemed to assess Clair. "Just like your ma." The old woman rubbed the hairs on her chin as if she were stroking a cat.

"Thank you." Clair still wasn't used to all the attention, but she was glad to hear someone speak of her mother.

Mrs. Plow glanced around the room. "Only been in this house a handful of times. Do you remember me looking after you when you had the chicken pox? Course, you were a young'un then. Mighty little. Oh, you was such a skinny little thing then. Made me wonder if your stepdad was taking proper care of you."

More childhood scenes came back to Clair—when she'd watched the comings and goings of Mrs. Plow from the attic window. The many times she'd hung out her laundry on the line and when she'd fed table scraps to a stray dog. And a few times when the older woman had waved at her and smiled. "Thank you for taking care of me when I was sick."

"Fiddlesticks." Mrs. Plow hunched over and grimaced. "I didn't come for no dainty gratitudes. Truth is. . .I didn't pay enough attention to you growing up. Should've done a whole lot more." She rubbed her gnarled hands together. "God told me to come back here and say something." She pointed her crooked finger in the air, looking upward. "I'll get to it."

Was Mrs. Plow talking to God or was she deranged? Clair waited for the woman to go on.

"Not sure what I'm supposed to say." Mrs. Plow pounded her fist into her palm. "He just said I needed to come."

They both sat in silence for a while, until Mrs. Plow started to chuckle. Then she looked at Clair. "Guess I shoulda got a clearer report before I found you."

Mrs. Plow sniggered so much, Clair started to laugh along with her. What an odd morning this was turning out to be.

Finally Mrs. Plow's laugh turned into a rasp and then a cough. "I'm getting kinda dry. Feels like my mouth is full of chicken feathers. Maybe I *will* have some tea."

Clair headed to the kitchen, where she got down her favorite teapot from the upper cupboard and a box of Darjeeling from the pantry. Mrs. Plow poked her head around the corner, making Clair jump.

"Didn't mean to scare you." The woman's smile showed a few missing teeth.

"It's all right. You're welcome to sit at the table."

"I know this is bad manners, but you got any food to go with the tea?" Mrs. Plow clutched her big handbag as she sat down.

Clair's heart went out to the woman. Even though Mrs. Plow had asked the question with a touch of humor, she looked hungry. Clair opened the refrigerator and pulled out some cheese and grapes. In the pantry, she located another muffin, along with some peanut butter.

When Clair had laid out their little feast, the older woman said grace and then began to take a few poised nibbles. Soon though, Mrs. Plow ate with gusto. After she'd gulped down several helpings of everything, the woman finally looked up from her plate. "I hadn't eaten in a while. Thank you, missy." She started to laugh again.

Clair joined in, grateful to have helped the woman.

Mrs. Plow glanced upward and said, "Okay, okay. I'll tell her, Lord. But I don't know what good it'll do her now. Be like stirring up the dregs and making everything dirty again." The old woman gave a wave toward heaven, clasped Clair's hand, and then paused.

"You can tell me. It's okay." Clair twisted the material on her shirt with her free hand, wondering what the woman was getting at.

Mrs. Plow pulled back, sighing. "After your ma passed on, your stepdaddy hurt so bad I think he blamed you for her death." She raised a wrinkled hand. "Don't you worry yourself, now. It was just his grief talking. You done nothing wrong."

Clair stared at the bare wall, trying to remember her stepfather's accusation, but no memory of it came to her. And yet she'd felt the friendless atmosphere that had permeated the house.

"You lived with him far too long, to my way of thinking."

"Eighteen. My stepfather died of an aneurysm when I was eighteen." The words escaped her lips in a whisper.

"I'm glad you got this house. It was your ma's home before he came. Not his. He didn't own nothing." Mrs. Plow's mouth twisted into a scowl.

Clair wondered what memories Mrs. Plow had of her mother. *Lord, help her to remember—about my mother.*

Mrs. Plow poured cream in her cup from the tiny pitcher then gulped the tea down, leaning her head way back to get the last drop. "Ahh, haven't had nothing that tasty in a long time," she said into the teacup. Then she looked back at Clair. "Your ma, oh, she was a good one. She knew the Lord, and she'd do anything for you." She patted Clair's hand. "I can see you got her kind spirit."

"Thank you." Clair took a sip of her tea. Mrs. Plow's words were sweeter than the little muffins set before them. *I remember now. My mother used to sing to me. She had the prettiest voice.* Clair remembered her smile—a lovely face leaning down to kiss her good night. And then her mother was gone. Forever.

"I'll just say it straight out." Mrs. Plow fidgeted in her chair, playing with the soiled lace on her sleeves. "I ain't never been one for regrets. Never been in my nature. But I am sorry about something."

"What do you mean?"

"I know what your stepdaddy did to you, how he ignored you. Saw it firsthand a time or two. He wasn't quite right in the head after your mama passed, God rest her soul. And he couldn't see beyond his own pain. That's true enough but was no excuse." Mrs. Plow's eyes fluttered as her shoulders sagged. "I know you spent a lot of time up in that little room with your mama's things."

Clair drew back, saying nothing. She wasn't sure if she wanted Mrs. Plow to continue. Until the recent conversation with Hudson, her past concerning her stepfather and the loneliness of the attic had been cloaked away in some dark corner of her mind. *Because when you name a thing. . .it truly exists. Then you have to deal with it.*

"First, I thought maybe you was just playing up there and peeking out the window like children do." Mrs. Plow grasped the tiny pitcher and drank the rest of the cream straight down. She wiped her mouth on her sleeve as she puckered her brows. "But you was up there too much, and you didn't look merry like the other kids. Then I heard a neighbor talking. Old Harvey Medville. He was over at your house, visiting, and he heard you up there, singing. So I know it was true. And I been blaming myself all these years for your loneliness. I shoulda stepped in and wrapped my arms around you, kissed away your tears."

"But it wasn't your fault or Mr. Medville's." Clair chewed on her lower lip.

The woman shook her head. "When a neighbor knows. . . and does nothing about it, well then, it's just the same as if they done it."

"But I don't blame you." Clair touched the woman's sleeve. "It's okay."

"Your stepdaddy could have put you in foster care." Mrs. Plow got a stern glint in her eye. "Or I coulda come over here and beat the living tar out of that man. Reminded him he had a daughter to care for."

The woman shook her head as her glare softened. "But I didn't, and I'm here to say, I knew a little of what you suffered. I never wanted you thinking his meanness was some fault of yours. You was such a fine child, sweet as jelly."

"He made sure I had the basic necessities," Clair said softly. "Food, clothing, a place to sleep at night. He just never knew how to give me the other things—love, affection. . ." Pain shot through Clair—one she'd never known. She'd always wondered if anyone had discovered her dismal plight. Now she knew for sure, and the sensations felt numbing and thorny at the same time. Was it anger that pierced her heart or merely a resignation that life didn't always offer justice? She knew some women might need counseling for having journeyed through such a pitiful youth, and yet she'd never felt compelled to see a therapist. Perhaps she'd been in denial or she'd pushed the past back into the attic like dead flowers pressed into a book.

"Basic necessities," Mrs. Plow huffed, balling up her fingers into a knotty fist, "wasn't enough." She let her fist thunder down on the table. "Not for an innocent child."

"I made it through okay." Clair gave her a sympathetic smile. "There wasn't anything you could have done."

Mrs. Plow pulled out a wad of tissues from the box on the table and blew her nose with vigor. She made a droning sound with her mouth and then patted Clair's cheek. "You have your mother's eyes. Just like the seraphim." She slipped the box of tissues into her enormous satchel and rose from her chair as if she'd left something heavy behind. "Well, I said my piece." She pointed to the food on Clair's plate. "You gonna eat those sweets?"

"No. Please take them."

Mrs. Plow opened her satchel wide and dumped the little plate of food into her bag. "I can't stay," she said with a sigh.

Clair's heart twisted within her at the thought of Mrs. Plow's leaving. "Will you come see me again? You're welcome anytime."

"Of course."

"Well, feel free. And, if you get the chance, come by and see me at work sometime. I run the little Christian bookstore in the River Market District. It's called Ima's."

"I'll do that, sweetie." Mrs. Plow limped to the front door.

Clair offered to pay for a taxi, but Mrs. Plow wouldn't hear of it. So, after hugging the older woman, Clair slipped a ten dollar bill in her pocket without her noticing—quite a sacrifice, considering her own current financial plight. But how could she do less? Mrs. Plow lumbered off down the sidewalk, looking tired but content.

Clair glanced at her watch and groaned. Somehow the time had gotten away from her. The church service was half over by now. No point in going today. She drew in a deep breath, pondering all that had happened this morning and feeling God's presence all around her. *He guides me in paths of righteousness. . .* The familiar words from her Bible reading urged Clair onward, motivated her to do something she'd never before had the courage to do.

Clair suddenly had an intense desire to see the attic—a place she'd avoided for years. Whether the need came out of curiosity or for closure, she didn't know, but maybe now, because of Mrs. Plow's words, the place would ring with truth instead of falsehood. And maybe one more sight of it would allow her to confront the soiled memories of her past and set them free.

She made her way through the same hallway she'd known all her life, but her heartbeat quickened as she carried herself up the dim and narrow staircase. With a trembling hand, she turned the doorknob and let the door swing open wide. She stumbled her way to the center of the room and pulled the chain above her head. Light filled the middle of the room, but shadows remained in every corner like murky vapors. A bare bulb swung from its chain as if the light itself had been hanged. *How did I endure this tomb-like place?*

Taking in a lungful of air, Clair looked around at the world she recognized all too well. *The attic.* The space smelled of mold and stale air, and except for a few old cartons of junk, the room appeared empty. She could almost hear a child singing—her own voice—but it was only memories haunting the air.

Clair sat down on a rope rug next to the dormer window where she'd spent hours at a time—watching, thinking, dreaming, singing, praying, and hoping someday to find a world beyond the gloomy walls and the lonesomeness it had brought her.

Her eyes misted over and, before she could convince herself to stop, a gush of tears came. She'd always found a reason not to cry, but this time no logic convinced her otherwise. The reality came to her full force—her stepfather hadn't wanted her or loved her. *Oh God, why did my mother have to die? What was the purpose in sending her to heaven so young? I needed her. My life would have been so different. I would have known love.*

Minutes seemed to flow into an unhurried stream as bits of the past came to her one by one. Clair wept softly. She leaned into the pain, knowing she could no longer drive it back. After her face felt washed clean with tears, she drew in a deep breath and turned her attention to the window.

A squirrel scampered over to the neighbor's sycamore tree and gazed upward. Then a precious little girl, dressed in violet overalls, tried catching the little animal. The squirrel scurried up the tree, making the child giggle.

Out of the blue, the little girl looked up at the dormer window, squinted, and then waved up at her as if she were a longtime friend. Clair rested her open palm against the warm glass and smiled. Amazingly, the child seemed to be the mirror image of herself when she'd been the same age. *Who is she?* The girl then skipped up the sidewalk as if she hadn't a care in the world. Perhaps that's how her heart felt now—just a little lighter. Clair stole one more glance, but the child had vanished.

What could this mean? Clair rested her head against the wall and wondered why she'd stayed in the same house all these years. Obligation? A sense of connectedness with the past, no matter how bleak? Or did she have a perverse need to continue her stepfather's tradition of neglect, thinking she somehow deserved it? Clair cringed at the thought.

Another one of Ima's sayings floated around in her head. "God gives us opportunities. He opens doors, but we have to decide to walk through them." She could almost hear Ima speaking to her. "Well, what are you going to do now, girly?"

Clair bowed her head and prayed for courage and wisdom. After a few minutes, she rose from the floor, and with determination, walked down the stairs as if she were being delivered into a new world.

thirteen

Clair knew where the telephone directory was, and she intended to use it. Ima had always talked about a Realtor friend of hers who had a reputation of being quite good. She scanned the yellow pages and found the familiar name—Elaine Kowalski.

After dog-earring the page, Clair closed the telephone book, and the words of the psalm flooded over her. *He restores my soul. He guides me in paths of righteousness for his name's sake.* Her awareness became more illuminated by the minute. The Lord—her Shepherd—had stirred her world, and she felt roused to action. Exhilaration coursed through her. *What shall I do next?*

She threw open all the kitchen windows—ones that had never been opened—and let the breeze blow through. She took in the fragrant air and accepted an unfolding truth. Even though she'd avoided the attic since her youth, she still hadn't escaped its hold on her. She knew now her spirit had been trapped up there all those years, pining away for permission to live. And to love.

She felt the mending touch all the way to her soul. Something shattered had been made whole. The trust and love once snatched away by human hands was divinely restored. God had used a unique and quirky woman named Harriet Plow to make it come to pass. All of heaven rejoiced with her, and she could almost hear the angels singing. She'd never been more ready to step into the light.

Early Monday morning, Clair signed a listing agreement with Elaine Kowalski and watched with pleasure as she placed a realty sign on her front lawn. Then Clair busied herself cleaning the house from top to bottom. Once she had her small abode spick-and-span, she looked around satisfied. *Hmm. Ancient and small, but clean.*

Knowing she had lots of work to do at the bookshop for the grand opening, Clair headed toward the bathroom to clean up. She carefully applied some of her new makeup and then slipped on a black and white pantsuit that Destinee had called chic.

An hour later when she arrived at the bookshop, she suddenly took note of the drab walls. Why hadn't she noticed the dull paint before—the color of rusty ship bottoms? *Hmm. Fresh paint would give the store a whole new look. Maybe a rich green would be nice—airy, soothing, and woodsy looking.* Just as she assessed the floors, a young woman with multi-colored, spiky hair pushed her way through the shop door with a large package.

"We're not open," Clair said. "At least not yet."

"Here for a delivery." The young woman smacked her gum between words. "Ms. . . .O'Neal."

"Thank you. You can just put the box on the counter."

The girl set the box down and then paused to chew her gum, blowing a mammoth bubble.

Clair handed the girl a tip and smiled. "I used to enjoy blowing bubbles, too. But I never got one as big as yours."

The girl handed Clair a couple of pieces of bubblegum and sauntered back outside.

Clair watched her go, feeling pleased with herself that she could talk so easily with a stranger. She popped a piece of the gum in her mouth and opened the newly delivered box. A smaller gift, wrapped in peach paper and a chiffon bow, sat nestled inside. *How lovely.* She wondered if Hudson had sent it.

Just as she lifted the gift out of the box and eased off the delicate bow, she heard the bell on the shop door again.

Hudson stood in the doorway. "Hi."

"Hello." Clair didn't hold back her joy. "Please come in."

"I realize you're busy getting ready—"

"It's okay. Really." She thought Hudson looked wonderful in his corduroys and his red-checked shirt. His boyish smile seemed to be in delightful contrast to his five-o'clock shadow.

Surprise also covered his handsome face. "You look more dazzling every time I see you," Hudson said. "This time it's in your eyes. How do you do that?"

Clair shrugged her shoulders. "Thank you." She held up the gift. "I got your present." *Oh dear.* In her enthusiasm, she might have goofed. *What if it's from someone else?*

Hudson walked closer to her. "I didn't send anything, but please, don't let me stop you." He stuffed his hands in his back pockets. "Let's see what it is."

Under the peach wrapping paper and folds of tissue sat an elegant bottle of perfume with a French name she couldn't pronounce. She knew little about such luxuries, but she could tell it was expensive—Rolex expensive.

"Looks like someone you know has excellent taste." Hudson's smile looked a little askew.

Clair opened the attached card. It simply read, *Glenn.* "It's from Glenn."

"Glenn Yves." Hudson lost his smile. All of it.

Should I explain or will it make things worse? "Glenn has taken me under his wing as my image coach. Years ago, someone helped him, and so he promised to help someone else in return." She swallowed hard. "*I'm* that person."

"Pretty generous of him." Hudson shifted his weight. "How did he choose you. . .if you don't mind my asking."

He had no hint of sarcasm in his voice, and yet Clair hoped he didn't think less of her for accepting the offer. She searched her mind for the right words. "I think I must have looked pitiful that night at the party."

"I didn't think you did." Hudson ran his finger along the counter. "I thought you looked. . .amazing."

Amazing? She would tuck that word away for later. "Thank you."

"Maybe he's really wanting to. . .you know. . .date you." He looked away. "Although I certainly can't blame him."

"Glenn sees me as a debt he must pay." Clair laced her hands together. "But I am grateful for his help." She realized she'd been smacking her gum, so she hid it in the side of her mouth.

"You could never be just an obligation. . .to anyone."

She saw the sweetest expression of concern in his eyes. "I will be careful." What a wonderful feeling, to have someone worried about her.

"Good." Hudson didn't look persuaded by her promise. "I also think you're somewhat naive where men are concerned." He rubbed his chin.

She could feel the familiar heat come to her face. "Maybe you could tell me what I need to know about them."

Hudson coughed and blinked.

Did I surprise him? Is that considered flirting? The sensation appeared to be enjoyable, yet disconcerting since she had no earthly idea how he would react to it. "Please."

Hudson's expression was a mix of bafflement and amusement. "Well, some men. . ." He turned away. "Not me, of course, but some men have expectations when they buy expensive gifts for a woman." He turned back to her with quiet intensity.

"Glenn is a fine Christian man." She crossed her arms and then uncrossed them. "In order to run this shop, I'll have to work with customers. He's helping me get over my shyness."

"Yes, I'll bet he is." He shook his head. "Oh boy. This really isn't my business." He raked his fingers through his hair. "But. . ." He pulled a guitar pick out of his pocket and passed it back and forth between his hands. "The reason I came. . . I wanted to invite you to go hiking with me. It's one of my favorite things. . .well, that and the Razorbacks." He grinned.

"Hiking?"

"Do you like to hike?" He had hope in his eyes.

"Yes. No. I mean, I've never been a hiker, but I would like to try."

"Well then." His face brightened. "One of my favorite places is Petit Jean State Park. I think you'll like it. So. . .how about Saturday?"

"Okay. Yes. *Am I smiling too much?*

Hudson beamed. "I'll pick you up at seven so we can get an early start. Just wear some comfortable clothes and sneakers. Okay?"

Clair nodded, wondering why she'd never hiked before. The thought of it sounded pleasant enough, especially with Hudson alongside her.

"By the way, how's the store coming along?" He leaned on the counter.

"I'm going to repaint." Clair pointed to one of the walls. "A woodsy green, maybe with a book border at the top. What do you think?"

Hudson nodded. "I'd love to help you."

Clair found it hard to accept help since she'd always done

everything for herself. "Well, I uh—"

"I mean it. I'm not like other people who just say things like that to be polite." He smiled then gestured toward the bottle. "Aren't you going to try on some of the perfume?"

"Oh. . .I guess." She removed the lid off the chunky bottle and dabbed a little of the pale amber liquid on her wrist. She took a long whiff of the scent. *Ohh my. Paradise in a bottle.* In a moment of boldness, she raised her wrist to him.

Hudson closed the short distance between them and leaned over her arm with a playful smile. He took in a deep breath. "Very nice. Maybe it *is* worth the money." He continued to hold her arm.

The combination of the stirring aroma and Hudson's warm touch made Clair's head go a little light. Suddenly embarrassed by her boldness, she eased away from him and held out a piece of bubblegum instead.

He accepted the gum with a grin, unwrapped it, and slipped it into his mouth. "Thanks. Well, I guess I should be going. Got to get back to my shop. I have a new hire, and she's like this cleaning lady on steroids. If she tries to organize my office, I'll never find anything again." He sauntered to the front door and then looked back at her. "Be careful now."

Clair gave him a little wave and wished she could have offered him coffee. She made a mental note to buy beans and filters.

"Let me know when you're ready to paint. I'll be happy to pick up a paint bucket and some brushes. Anything you need."

"Thanks. That would be great." Clair's hand went to her heart. *What an attentive and caring man.*

"You're welcome." Hudson seemed pleased.

"Okay." Clair watched him through the window as he strode

in the direction of his guitar shop, chewing his bubblegum with great enthusiasm. Out of the blue, Glenn appeared, walking right by Hudson. They exchanged polite nods as Glenn reached for the handle on the shop door. The last sight of Hudson was a frown directed at Glenn.

Oh dear.

fourteen

Glenn came through the door with his usual flair, once again wearing a gleaming smile and tailored garments, which made the most of his physique. "Hello."

"Hi." Clair reminded herself to thank him for his generous gift.

He glanced out the window. "Hudson stopped by, I see." His comment came out heavily, as if it were burdened with questions.

She nodded.

"Ah." Glenn frowned, smoothing his tie. "Looks like I'm better at what I do than I want to be."

Clair wasn't sure what he meant, so she just let the comment go.

"If Hudson wants to make it big in the music business, he needs to buy some new clothes." Glenn crossed his arms.

Clair did her best not to respond.

"I'm going to break my own social rules here and ask you something impolite." Glenn cleared his throat. "Are you dating that guy?"

What should I say? "We're going hiking."

"Hiking?" Glenn said the word as if it were vulgar. "Why hike when there are spas and fitness centers? Besides, you aren't the type."

"Thank you for the perfume. I've never had anything so. . ." *I shouldn't say expensive.* "Anything so elegant. But you shouldn't have spent so—"

"My mentor was generous with me, and I intend to be generous as well."

Clair noticed a yearning kind of expression in his eyes. *Perhaps he's ill.*

He moved toward her. "By the way, I came by to take you to lunch. . .if you're free. Today we'll be discussing proper attire. Also, we'll talk about how to deal with the media."

"Media?" Clair tried not to look panicky.

"Well, I'm sure you'll want to announce your opening. Set up some book signings. Talk it up with the media." He made a gesture with his hands. "You know, create some buzz."

She took in a deep breath and made a point to look at Glenn. "Okay."

"By the way, your black-and-white outfit is a good choice."

Clair smiled. "It's all because of your kindness."

"I disagree." He arched an eyebrow. "A rose is still a rose even when it hasn't bloomed yet."

She wanted to say something clever back, but her mind became a blank sheet of paper. She chewed on her lower lip, but then remembering Glenn's instruction, she stopped herself.

"Listen, I have a client to visit with for a few minutes, but I could meet you at the Harbor Inn Café at noon." Glenn glanced at his watch. "Will that work for you?"

"Yes."

"See you then." He maneuvered his way through the standing bookshelves and tables and then slipped out the door.

Clair still couldn't get over the fact that a man as remarkable and refined as Glenn Yves had decided to mentor her. She picked up a broom nearby and began to sweep the floor as she thought about all the recent events in her life. She wondered how she'd ever get her shop opened with all the sudden attention. *But I enjoy being cared for.* In fact, she wondered what would happen if all the benevolence toward her suddenly stopped. Would the loneliness feel worse than it had before?

Ima had always said, "You can't depend on other people for your happiness. Just make sure things are right between you and God and then the other joys will come." Clair thought her friend's words sounded like good advice, so she dismissed any more melancholy thoughts.

Just as Clair had swept up a sizable pile of dirt, the door opened again. A woman exploded into the shop, looking annoyed and in a hurry. *It's Leslie, the author, from the party—Hudson's sister!* Clair dropped her broom. "Hi. It's nice to—"

"It's Clair, right?"

"Yes. I'm—"

Leslie fiddled with her earring until she grimaced. "You don't look like the same woman I met at my party. You've had your hair done or something."

"Yes. I went to a spa, and—"

"I've stopped by to see about doing a book signing." Leslie made a dramatic gesture with her hand, nearly knocking over a display ornament.

"O–oh?" Clair stammered. "Well, we're undergoing renovations right now. Besides, Ima's the one who always takes care of book signings and she's—"

"Yes, I heard about that. So sorry. But I thought perhaps holding a book signing would help increase your business. When you're ready, of course."

What a kind gesture. Clair fumbled around, looking for the calendar. As she located it, Leslie continued to talk.

"I, um, saw you with my brother at the Silver Moon Café the other evening."

"Yes." Clair couldn't help but smile. "I had a wonderful time."

"Seemed a little odd, that's all." Leslie shrugged.

"Oh?" Clair looked over at Leslie, trying to make sense of her meaning.

"Well. . ." Leslie fidgeted with her hair. "Hudson has been involved with Tara for so long now, it's just. . .different to see him take an interest in someone else."

Clair lowered her gaze to the pile of dirt, clutching the calendar in her hands. "But I—"

"I know you can understand the love a sister has for her brother. I simply want what's best for Hudson." Leslie strolled around a table of books.

"Oh?" Leslie's perfume seemed to fill the entire store. Clair pinched her nose to keep from sneezing.

Leslie's green eyes took on a more intense hue. "Tara's a great girl. A good friend. And it's been a lot of fun to watch her relationship with Hudson blossom like it has."

I'm breathing too fast. Clair's head went wobbly. "But what if Hudson doesn't care for her. . .in that way?" She'd blurted out the question before she'd thought of the ramifications of such a bold query.

Leslie gazed at her fingernails and then looked back at Clair. "Men rarely know what they really want. At least, that's been my experience." She adjusted the collar on her blouse.

"But he wrote a song for me." The moment Clair spoke the words she wished she'd kept them to herself.

"Yes." Leslie set her purse down on a shelf and ambled about the store as if she were looking for something. "I heard the song. There's no doubt it's beautiful." She shrugged and smiled. "But that's what songwriters do—write songs when they're moved. I'm sure you've inspired him, but you see, he's touched and stirred by everything around him." She held up a novel.

"He's an artist. It's what we do—use the things around us for our work."

Clair closed her mouth and released her hold on the calendar, setting it on the table. Leslie hadn't come here today to talk about a book signing. Not even close. A sickening feeling churned in Clair's stomach. What happened? Could the beginning now be the end? *No tears, Clair. No tears.*

All the recent hopes and joys were disappearing like Cinderella's coach—midnight had clearly come. The girl who had always been known as nobody would now make her quiet exit. She chewed on her lower lip until she flinched in pain.

Leslie set the novel back on the shelf with a thump and then glared at the bottle on the counter. "Oh, don't you love that brand of perfume? I have the very same bottle! Glenn Yves sent it to me. You met him at my party, I think."

"Y–yes."

Leslie fingered the bottle with a dreamy look in her eyes then glanced at her watch. "I should probably be going. I've got an appointment." She took a few steps toward the door then looked back with a whimsical smile. "I'll, um, call you about that book signing. We'll work out the details."

Sure we will.

As soon as Leslie left, Clair shut the door and made sure the closed sign was in place. Then she wilted into a nearby chair, deep in thought. Would she really be forced to stop going out with Hudson? Life had not only become too fast, it'd also become peopled and problematic. How had she gotten into such a dilemma? All because she'd agreed to replace Ima at a party.

A banging on the shop window jolted her back to reality. A stranger had stopped in front of the shop and had apparently pounded on the glass. The woman stared in at her as if she were an animal in a cage. Surely the lady could read the sign on the door.

Clair slumped to the floor. *Oh dear God, what am I doing?* Did she even have the temperament for running a store? Would she really be able to handle all the challenging customer demands? *And is dating this difficult for everyone else?*

Clair pulled herself from the floor and shut off the lights. Without intending to, she knocked over a chair. The deed felt unexpectedly good, so then one by one, she knocked all the decorative hats off the walls. Then she stared at the bare spaces. *What am I doing?* She'd never been aggressive or destructive in her life.

Then the realization hit her full force. *I care about him. I have feelings for Hudson.* Just hearing Leslie's comments about Tara caused a gripping pain in her chest. Was she right? Would Hudson be better off with someone as polished and refined as Tara? Surely Leslie thought so.

Clair lowered herself to the floor again and scooted under the ledge of the counter. She rested her chin on her knees in the quiet darkness of the shop. As she sat there and prayed, her stomach growled. *Hunger. Food. Lunch. Glenn. Oh no.* She'd forgotten to meet Glenn at the Harbor Inn Café. What would he think of her?

Moments later, the bell jingled over the front door. Who could that be? Clair decided to stay put. *Maybe it's Leslie returning to tell me all the men in Little Rock are off limits.* Her last thought surprised her. She'd rarely ever entertained sarcasm, and that was definitely sarcastic!

"Clair? Where are you?"

It's Glenn's voice. "I'm down here." She started to scramble to her feet.

Glenn peeked around some shelving. "There you are. No. Don't get up. I'll come down to you."

"But your suit. It'll get all—"

"Stay put." He took off his jacket and tossed it on the counter. Then he sat down on the floor next to her.

Amazingly, he didn't even ask why she was sitting on the floor. "I'm so sorry I forgot about lunch," she said.

He seemed to study her expression. "When you were late, I decided to come and find you."

They sat for a while without speaking. For the first time, Clair felt truly comfortable with Glenn. He seemed so out of character to just be sitting on the floor with her, staring into space like he had nothing better to do.

"May I be honest?" Glenn asked.

"Yes."

"You have some joy in your eyes since I met you at the party, but I think you're still living as if you don't really matter."

Clair looked away. "It takes time to rewrite a book."

"I'm going to ask you something personal, okay?" Glenn draped his arms over his knees.

"Go ahead."

"What are you most afraid of—above all else?"

Had she ever really thought about the subject from that angle? "Well. . .I wouldn't want to pass through this world without ever touching another life. I wouldn't want my shyness to keep me so incapacitated that I couldn't live the life I was meant to live."

He shook his head and smiled. "You know exactly what you want, and you know what's holding you back. Most people don't have a clue."

Clair wondered why she couldn't have been more articulate with Leslie.

Glenn smoothed his gold tie. "Clair. I like your name."

"I always thought it sounded old-fashioned." She suddenly noticed his scent—the heady smell of a life lived sumptuously. She realized some women would give anything to live such a life and to live it with him.

"No. Your name has a pure and gentle sound. . .like rain." His voice trailed off as he lowered his gaze to her lips. The shop door opened, making the bell jangle hysterically again. "She's closed," Glenn hollered to the intruder.

The rhythmic clomping of high heels grabbed Clair's attention. Maybe she'd need to make her closed sign bigger.

The woman, whoever she was, kept clomping until she stood in front of them. Leslie Mandel stared down at them with her hands on her hips.

Clair's heart skipped a beat.

Glenn looked up with surprise. "What are you doing here?"

"I forgot my purse." Leslie snatched up her bag from behind a stack of books. She stared at them with huge eyes as if she were watching a horror movie. "Well well well. Glenn, I wondered where you've been. Guess this answers that question."

Glenn shrugged as he said, "Clair and I are just sitting here talking."

"Right." Leslie stormed out the door, slamming it so hard the glass shuddered in the window.

"Hmm. Not good." Glenn groaned. "As you know, Leslie is a past client of mine." He leaned his fist against his chin. "I've never led her to believe we were anything more than friends."

Clair touched the sleeve of his jacket. "She cares for you."

"I suppose." He shook his head. "I never meant to hurt her."

"I'm sure you didn't."

Glenn let out a lungful of air. "Tell me, Clair. If you were in my situation, what would *you* do to put a closure to this?"

As the irony of what Glenn asked became clear, the moment turned to agony. She would soon be faced with the same situation, since she had no intention of allowing herself to cause a rift in Hudson's relationship with his sister. *Not ever.* Family was essential to life, and she would sacrifice her own happiness for it.

After a long pause, Clair said, "I think I would tell her as tenderly as possible."

fifteen

Hudson and Clair strolled out of the lodge at Petit Jean State Park and headed down the path, which led to a ridge overlooking the Arkansas River Valley. Hudson drank in the sight—the sky mingled with the hills in layer upon layer of azure blue. *Nice.*

"I've always loved Arkansas," Clair said. "It's so beautiful." She took a few steps closer to the edge. "But I had no idea this was here."

"I've been here many times." Hudson pointed straight ahead. "Right over there is Mount Nebo. There're some pretty interesting legends and history here." He took in a deep breath of fresh air. "I really think early spring is the best time of year. Life is sort of hatching out. . .lots of promise."

He glanced over at Clair. On the drive to the park, she'd seemed pleased to be with him, but he noticed in spite of her more outgoing manner, some kind of anxiety lingered in her countenance. In fact, during the week, he'd wondered why she hadn't taken him up on his offer to help her paint the bookshop. "I'm glad the weather warmed back up for us." He smiled. "And I'm glad you dressed in sneakers and jeans. You'll be glad you did. It's a two-mile hike."

Clair grinned back at him. "You're scaring me. Is the hike down to the falls strenuous?"

"You'll do just fine. I promise."

As they descended the rock stairs, Hudson held her hand to steady her. A soothing warmth pulsed through his fingers.

Clair hopped down a step or two ahead of him.

He watched her, pleased she seemed to be enjoying herself. With the exception of a few tourists, they had the place to themselves. He suddenly remembered a brief mention of rain in the day's forecast. *Maybe the threat of a rainstorm kept the visitors at bay.*

She stopped suddenly. "I hear a waterfall."

"It's right down there." Hudson pointed to the left. "This is just a small one. But one time I wrote a song sitting right over there."

"Really?" Clair climbed over the rocks to the little falls and sat down on a boulder. She remained quiet for a moment and then said, "I value your passion for composing music. I mean, to make something beautiful that has never existed before. . .to have it manifest itself from your creative mind must be. . . unspeakable rapture."

"Unspeakable rapture?" He couldn't help but smile at her word choices. Everything about Clair warmed his heart, right down to her vocabulary.

She lowered her fingers into the clear, rushing water. "Do you suppose that's how God felt when He made all of this?"

"Maybe." He sat down next to her. "I don't know for certain. I'm not God. Although I know a couple of people in the music business who *think* they are."

Clair chuckled.

Hudson wished he hadn't devalued an awesome moment by making a joke of it, but his mind couldn't seem to stay on course. He just wanted to take Clair into his arms and explain how he really felt. He restrained himself again, knowing the moment wasn't right.

"You know, I don't really create something from nothing," he said. "I have life to inspire me." Should he give her a glimpse into his heart? "And I have *you* to inspire me." He noticed a flash of pain shadow her face. *What could be troubling her?*

Hudson rose, gazing at the view. Like ancient monuments, the bluffs and hills never seemed to change with time. He glanced back at Clair, wondering if through the years he'd ever passed her on the streets of Little Rock, not knowing who she was—not knowing she'd be the one to change his life. After a moment or two longer, Hudson said, "Tell me when you're ready to move on."

"I am." She dusted herself off and headed back to the main trail.

He followed her, pondering her silence.

After a while, they reached the bottom of Cedar Creek Canyon and then hiked along the water's edge. Hudson took in the sounds—the burbling noises of the creek and the occasional chirp of a small bird. Even though the ground was coated with brown leaves, tufts of green grass sprang up here and there and the trees flourished with new green buds. Glancing upward, he could see a jagged outcrop of charcoal sandstone against a velvet blue sky. He'd grown to love the canyon and the way it helped him relinquish the day and lose himself in the natural world.

Clair stopped to look at a moss-covered log. "You know, you have a very gifted voice."

That was certainly unexpected. "Thank you." *One compliment from her is better than a hundred pieces of flattery.*

"Have you always loved music?" Clair brushed her hand against the tiny yellow flowers peeking out from the leaves.

"Yeah. Even when I was a little guy, my parents said I always tried to make musical instruments out of junk. You know. . .buckets were drums and seeds in empty toilet paper rolls were maracas. That sort of thing. Believe me, our house was pretty noisy when I was growing up."

Clair chuckled.

"But I've always liked the way music changes people—makes them pause to think about something else. Something that lifts up above the roar. . .to hear again." Hudson stuffed his hands in his pockets. "Sorry. I'm rambling."

"No, not at all. I think life would be unbearable without music. It. . .ushers us into the presence of God."

He watched as her face lit up with a fervor that surprised him. *She really does understand.*

When the path narrowed a bit, Hudson let her walk ahead of him. After a while, he could hear the thundering waters.

When Cedar Falls came into view, they stood still, taking in the beauty of it. The water fell nearly a hundred feet over a shelf of weathered rock. Mist formed at the base of the falls, creating a rainbow effect.

"It's wonderful. Can we get closer?"

Hudson pointed to the left. "Why don't we climb over there and sit under the overhang?"

They maneuvered around the uneven terrain. Hudson wiped off one of the powdery boulders and they sat down.

"This is a perfect spot." She clasped her hands together.

He gazed at her and then looked up at the falls. The waters crashed down before them and collected in a small lake, as if nature had given it a respite, before moving on again through the canyon.

Clair turned toward him. "I was just wondering. . .about your shop. Do you enjoy running a business?"

He didn't need to think long on that question. "Not really. But I do enjoy teaching the kids. . .watching their excitement. . . seeing their progress. Owning a business is a ton of work. And because of the shop, I don't have much time to perform."

"Do you want to perform full-time someday?"

"Sure. But right now, I need the income from both. I would like my songs to reach more people, but it takes promotion, which in turn takes a lot of cash. I guess you could say the music is the beauty and the promotion is the beast."

Clair didn't respond but just seemed to listen quietly. Hudson decided to continue. "And there're other pressures. My sister, Leslie, has always been an overachiever. She got published at twenty, which is very young. She was always a go-getter through high school, too. Cheerleader, president of the student council, prom queen, you name it."

Clair appeared to consider what he'd said. "Weren't you prom king?"

Hudson laughed. "No way. I had thick-rimmed glasses, acne, and a severe case of the chubbies."

She shook her head. "I can't imagine that."

"It's true. And I think I always compared myself to Leslie, strange as that seems." He shook his head. "Maybe it's just her excessive interest in my life, my business."

"What do you mean?" Clair's expression grew more curious.

Hudson shrugged. "She's always wanted to remake me. Fix my hair, dress me, pair me up with just the right girl—that kind of thing."

"Ah."

"I think she believes I'm meant for bigger things in the music business than teaching a few guitar lessons and singing in a café. I don't have any record deals, so sometimes I feel like I've let her down."

Clair looked as if she might say something but then didn't.

"I think it's why some of my songs tend to run a little on the melancholy side. I guess you could say there are things from my childhood that still haunt me." He gave her a warm smile. "So, even though I have no idea of the kind of isolation you had growing up, I knew how it felt to be on the outside looking in. Hey, that'd be a good song title, wouldn't it? 'The Outside Looking In.'"

"Yes, it is good."

Hudson picked up a rock chip and skipped it across the water.

"I feel some pressure, too. . .about the store," Clair said, breaking the silence between them. "But I don't want to disappoint Ima."

"I know you loved Ima, but she wouldn't want you to run the store if that wasn't what you were created to do. Would she?"

Clair looked at him. "I'm not sure, but I don't think so."

Oh, how he loved those brown eyes full of sweetness. Hudson handed her a flat stone to toss.

She pulled back and threw the stone, making it light upon the water like a dragonfly.

"That was a good one." Hudson sat down on a rock near her.

"Since no one is here, would you sing to me?" Clair asked.

"Only if you want to. But I love to hear you sing."

"Okay." Hudson took in a deep breath and began to sing the first verse of "Amazing Grace." After he'd finished, he stopped and said, "Do you know the last verse?"

"Yes."

"Will you sing it with me?"

Clair shook her head. "No. I don't think so."

"But we're alone—just you and me and God. It'll be okay." Hudson began singing the last verse and then Clair joined him. At first she faltered and sang so softly he could barely hear her. And then something astonishing happened. She straightened her shoulders and sang more loudly. Really sang. Her voice rose up, sweet and clear as it echoed through the canyon. In fact, her voice sounded so extraordinary he almost stopped singing. Had she had lessons growing up? Where had she learned to sing like that? He felt awestruck and tried not to stare at her.

When they'd released the last word of "Amazing Grace" up to the heavens, he felt exhilarated. And something else. The very air around them seemed charged with expectancy. Hudson paused to compose his words. "Where. . .did you learn to sing so beautifully?" He stood up and touched her arm.

Clair lowered her head. "I. . .well. . .as I mentioned, I sang in the attic. I sang every song I heard on the radio. And sometimes I would make up my own songs."

Hudson wasn't sure what to do next. He hadn't heard a voice like hers since. . .well, he couldn't really remember when he'd heard such an exquisite and unique voice. "Has anyone ever told you that you have a remarkable gift?"

"No."

"You mean you've never sung for anyone?"

"No. Only when I'm alone." Clair looked away. "Or at church. But there, I'm just one voice among hundreds. No one would single me out, and you would certainly never catch me singing solo."

"But why?" Hudson couldn't fathom a voice likes hers left undiscovered.

She sat down on a nearby rock and gave him a puzzled smile. "I'm not sure anymore."

"I'm sorry for badgering you with so many questions. It's just. . .well. . .God has given you such an extraordinary talent." He took in a deep breath, still trying to absorb what he'd heard.

"Thank you." Clair brought her shoulder up to her cheek in a shy shrug.

"I really enjoyed singing with you just now." Hudson sat down next to her.

"I liked it, too." Even as Clair shared those encouraging words, her eyes seemed to be expressing two conflicting messages—joy and sorrow.

There were so many things he still wanted to ask her, and yet the moment seemed to be leading them elsewhere. "Clair?"

"Yes?"

Surely she didn't think they were just friends. "I would like to. . ." Like the leaves aloft around them, Hudson's voice floated away on the breeze.

"What were you going to say?"

"You've got to know."

She shook her head.

Clair seemed so innocent in so many ways—so honest and uncomplicated—he found it impossible not to adore her. He reached over to her and swept a lock of hair over her slender shoulder. She didn't pull away. Good sign. *If I kiss her would she run?* Probably not. Would she slap him? Never. But he might see disappointment in her lovely face, and that response he couldn't take.

In spite of Hudson's reservations, he took hold of her hand and, while cradling it, lowered his head and tenderly kissed the palm of her hand.

Clair's eyelids fluttered shut.

He took her reaction for a positive sign. Not wanting to waste another second, he lifted her chin and leaned over to kiss her.

sixteen

Hudson traced Clair's cheek with his fingertip, gazing at her lovingly. Did she have mist in her eyes? "What are you thinking?"

"About your kiss." She smiled as she folded her hands in her lap.

"And what exactly were you pondering about that kiss?" He covered her hands with his.

Clair's expression became wistful. "I was thanking God my very first kiss was with you."

Did she really say *first* kiss? *But Clair is thirty-one years old.* Suddenly feeling protective, he rose up and pulled her into his arms. "How can that be possible?"

Clair reddened. "I'm afraid it's true."

"Then. . .I feel honored."

She relaxed in his arms and rested her head on his shoulder.

How could a woman like Clair go unnoticed for so long? The idea could not be understood.

Hudson continued to hold Clair, enjoying the closeness and her steady breathing. So constant and gentle—qualities he hadn't seen an abundance of in the music business. Then a vision came to him—one of her singing with him on stage. *Should I ask her? What would she say?* "I know this might seem sudden, but would you ever consider singing with me at the Silver Moon? I already know people would love your voice."

"Oh, I don't know." She drew away from him and sat down, gripping the rock underneath her as if it could fly away.

Clair's gaze seemed so far away, he wondered if he'd ever be invited into her world. Hudson stared back out at the waters cascading over the top of the chasm and thought of his own wild fears of performing. "The first time I got up on stage I actually passed out." He chuckled. "They had to drag me off the stage like a side of beef."

A grin eased across her face. "I don't believe you."

"Yep. Made a total fool of myself. And then the second time I performed, I threw up. And I'd just had an enormous lunch. I won't go into the details, but that incident was even more humiliating because I was awake to see the audience's reaction."

Clair's hand went to her mouth. "What was it—the audience's reaction?"

"Mostly horror." He laughed.

"Then why did you continue?"

"Because making music is what I was created to do. And I knew I wouldn't be content until I fulfilled the desire of my heart." He shuffled his feet and grinned. "And I guess some in my family won't be content until I get a record deal."

A hint of sadness came back to Clair's eyes, but Hudson decided to put his concerns on hold. He picked up a rock near his shoe and considered the sheets of shale all layered together into one stone. *Time put this rock together, and time will take it apart.* He didn't like where his thoughts were roaming, so he looked back at Clair, smiling at her and absorbing the miracle of her. He took hold of her hand and brought it to his lips.

"You know. . .I think you are a fine man." Clair gently removed her hand from his grasp.

Hudson liked hearing the compliment but wondered why Clair pulled away. He handed the gray stone to her, hoping to lighten the mood. Her hands appeared to be shaking. "You're trembling. Are you cold?"

Clair slowly shook her head. "How can I say this to you?"

"This sounds more like an ending than a beginning. What's wrong?"

She lowered her gaze. The rock slipped from her hand and clattered against the other stones.

"What is this?" When Clair said no more, Hudson realized she didn't want to pursue a relationship or even continue the conversation. "Was it because I asked you to sing?"

"No. Don't ask me why." Clair turned away. "Please."

"But your kiss. I thought you—" He stopped when Clair shook her head. Swallowing back the lump in his throat, he asked, "W–were you kissing me good-bye?" As if someone had punched him, he felt the air empty from his lungs.

She nodded.

His mind reeled with the truth. *God help me. What did I do? Why is she rejecting me?* Disappointment and confusion tore through him.

Thunder rumbled around them. A blue-black horizon crowned with boiling white clouds loomed near. *How could the storm have crept up so quickly?* Streaks of lightning, blinding and jagged, exploded all around them. He refocused his attention from the inner tempest churning inside him to the approaching storm. "We'd better go now before it pours."

They alternated walking swiftly and jogging through the canyon. It seemed like an eternity before they made it up to the park building and then safely into his pickup. The moment they shut the doors, the rain came down in heavy sheets.

"Quite a storm. I'll get you home." Hudson looked over at her, so very near him yet so far away. "I don't want this to be good-bye." Hudson tried to keep the desperation out of his voice, but be felt the raw emotion in each word. "If we could just. . ." His voice faded away.

Clair's face appeared full of compassion as she reached over and kissed him on the cheek.

Or was it pity? What could have gone wrong? For a few moments he'd seen love in her eyes. He rebuked himself for asking her to sing with him at the café. Had he frightened her or was there something else at play? A man named Glenn Yves? He pulled out of the parking lot, wounded and distressed, but determined to find out what or who had turned her away from his love.

seventeen

Monday morning, Clair dragged herself into the shop, feeling worn out and disheartened. Over the weekend, a family had made a low offer on her house. She'd told Elaine to accept it, since the home was old and in need of repairs.

But her home meant little to her compared to her feelings for Hudson. She'd removed herself from his life. Even though the closure seemed to be the right thing to do for his career, it didn't feel right in her heart.

In her years spent alone, she'd learned how to close herself off to pain. But now, only weeks after she'd crept out of her shell, the world had crushed her newly exposed feelings. And never had her singing felt so meaningful as in those few moments with Hudson.

What am I to do? I have no mother to talk to. And I don't feel right about talking to Glenn about it. The situation would be awkward, but she wasn't sure why since Glenn was only a mentor and friend.

Clair plopped down on a stool behind the counter and stared at her to-do list for the store's grand opening. First, she needed to get her car repaired so she'd be able to run all the necessary errands. Although she hated to take money from the bookstore funds, she also knew there was no other way to accomplish her goals. As she decided which car repair place might give her the best deal, a woman entered the shop.

"Yoo-hoo," she called out.

"I'm closed. . .for now."

"Oh, honey, I know." The woman stepped inside. A red feather on top of a purple hat waggled above the bookracks as she made her way toward Clair.

"May I help you?"

The effervescent fifty-something stopped near the counter. She had skin the color of cocoa, dancing black eyes, and a smile as warm as hotcakes off the griddle. "I don't know if you remember me, but I attended Ima Langston's funeral. She was a dear friend of mine."

"Yes, I do remember you now."

"I'm Mabel Sugar." She laughed. "My momma had a fine sense of humor, didn't she?"

Clair chuckled with her. "You had the lovely spray of lavender flowers. I know Ima would have liked them. It was her favorite color." Clair strode over to Mabel and reached out her hand. "I'm Clair O'Neal."

Mabel shook Clair's hand with enthusiasm. "It's mighty fine to meet you." Mabel crisscrossed her hands over her heart. "I'm here. . . Well. . .the good Lord and I have an offer for you."

"Offer?"

"For the shop. I know you own the shop now. Ima's sister told me. And well, I would love to make you an offer to buy your shop."

"But the shop isn't for sale."

"Let me just say this, and then I'll go." Mabel took off her purple hat and patted it against her leg. "When I was growing up my momma read to me all the time on our front porch swing. She always said the bookstore held its head higher than the candy shop, because cultivating the mind and feeding the soul were superior to nourishing my cavities."

They both chuckled.

"Your mother sounds very wise," Clair said.

"Oh yes, she was." Mabel became somber. "And I always listened to my momma. I've saved some money, and now I hope to buy a bookstore right here in Little Rock. It's where I grew up. I love this city. We have the friendliest people in the world here. So this is where I'll have my store." She looked around. "I knew Ima's intentions. In fact, I'm the one who gave her the idea for renovating the store. I just wondered, honey, if this isn't your dream, then I would love to make it mine."

"You want to buy the business from me?" Clair repeated the words to let the news settle in.

"My offer would be more than fair." Mabel fiddled with the clasp on her purse. "The good Lord has been bighearted with me, so I can afford to be generous. If you have a few moments, I would like to speak with you about the particulars."

"Yes, I have the time."

Clair was thankful she had brought a coffeemaker to the shop as over a fresh-brewed cup, Mabel made her more-than-generous offer. She couldn't help but wonder if this was more confirmation that she really wasn't meant to continue with the shop.

"I'll leave you now." Mabel put her hat back on. "Give you some time to ruminate, as momma always said."

"I will. . .think about it. Seriously." Clair shook Mabel's hand again. "Thank you for coming."

"You are so welcome. Here's my card." Mabel handed Clair a handsome-looking business card with gold lettering. It read, "Mabel Sugar, Realtor," and gave her contact information.

Clair wondered how it would feel to change midcourse to follow a lifelong dream.

"Just pray about it, honey." Mabel ambled to the front door. "God will show you the way." She walked out the door, her talk turning into singing. " 'And lead us to the Promised Land.' "

Clair wilted into a soft chair. Life was speeding along like a locomotive. She'd most likely lost Hudson's companionship forever, she'd soon have to move out of her house, and now Ima's friend had forced her to question whether she was ever meant to run a bookstore. Panic rose inside her.

❧

Many hours and prayers later, Clair ran some much-needed errands for the shop. By late afternoon, she drove home with her newly repaired car, which was something she hadn't been able to do in some time. *Oh, the luxury of a working vehicle.*

The moment Clair shut her front door, her stomach growled. Instead of rummaging around in her fridge for something to eat, she found herself showering and dressing for the evening. She picked a dress from her new wardrobe— a simple but elegant black dress.

Some part of her wanted to go back to the way things were weeks earlier; hiding would certainly be easier. But Clair knew those days could never be again. Her life had finally moved on from the attic. And yet, she felt more alone than ever. Had she made a terrible mistake saying good-bye to Hudson?

There's one way to find out. He's playing at the Silver Moon Café. Tonight.

eighteen

Hudson lifted his guitar from his stand and settled down under the spotlights at the Silver Moon Café. "Good evening. I'm Hudson Mandel."

After waiting for the usual applause, he gazed out over the heavy crowd. The house lights were still high enough to see some of the people. Tara Williamson and her family were in the middle, beaming and clapping as always. But when he scanned the left side, he caught a glimpse of his sister, Leslie, talking to someone—someone who looked just like Clair. In fact, when she turned a bit, he could tell the woman was indeed Clair.

Hudson felt so startled to see her he nearly forgot where he was. "Clair," he accidentally said out loud. Some girls from the audience yelled, "We love you, Hudson," which shocked him back to reality. He decided since he'd said her name, he would sing her song. "This first one. . .is for someone very special."

Perspiration beaded up on his forehead, and his heartbeat picked up its rhythm. Hudson hadn't felt so unnerved since he'd first started performing. *Breathe.* He hugged the guitar and positioned his hands. The song began softly as a hush swept over the audience. He knew he had them, but he really hoped he had the attention of the woman he'd written the song for.

When Hudson finished, he thanked everyone and gave his signature salute, but all that occupied his thoughts were Clair's presence and the possibility that she'd changed her mind. He certainly hoped so as he scanned the audience, looking for her again. He spotted Clair by the exit, walking out with someone. *Glenn Yves.*

Hmm. Maybe his sister knew something about it, since he'd seen her talking to Clair earlier. He hurried down the steps and sat down next to Leslie. "I noticed you were talking to Clair."

Leslie cocked her head at her brother. "Well, hi to you, too."

"Sorry. It's just. . .well. . .Clair left suddenly with Glenn."

A twinge of something dark passed over Leslie's face. "Well, a girl has a right to leave with anyone she chooses. They can't *all* worship you."

"Come on, Leslie. You were talking to her. What did you say?"

Leslie shook her head and tugged on the corner of his shirt. "You really need to let me help you shop for some new clothes." She turned her attention to the sautéed vegetables on her plate.

"*What* did you say to Clair?"

"Are you insinuating I ran her off?"

"Not necessarily. Did you?"

Leslie looked annoyed. "I met her when she came to my party. I just told her how surprised I was to see her."

Hudson leaned toward her. "That's all?" He raised an eyebrow, thinking she looked a little guilty of something.

Leslie took a sip of water and then stared at him over her glass. "You really do care for her?"

Perhaps I should just tell her. "I want to marry her."

"Don't say it so loudly." Leslie cupped her hand near her mouth. "Tara's right over there. She can hear you."

Hudson rose. "I really don't care who hears it. I would have said it from the stage if I thought it would have made Clair stay."

"Well, maybe you should let her go. It wasn't meant to be, Huddy."

He let out a slow breath to calm his frustration. "I'm a grown man now." He splayed his fingers on the table, leaning toward her. "And please stop calling me Huddy."

"But it's so cute."

"I'd like to put childish things away. . .if you don't mind." Hudson gave her his most sober look.

"Okay." Leslie held up her hands wildly in mock surrender. "I get the message."

Hudson slowly nodded. "Very good." He gave his sister a quick hug and headed back to the stage.

Knowing Clair had left with Glenn weighed heavily on his spirit. *She must have meant her good-bye.* But he knew two questions would burn in his mind all evening. *Why had she come alone, and then why did she leave with Glenn?* Or had something else happened, and he just didn't have all the facts?

❧

Early the next morning, Clair slowly unlocked the bookshop door and wondered why such a simple task seemed so tiring. But the previous evening had been quite an emotional ride.

On a whim she'd wanted to watch Hudson perform—to make certain she hadn't made the worst mistake of her life by driving him away. But Leslie had been there, too, and she'd acted very surprised to see her. Her greeting hadn't been the happy kind of surprise like most people experience among friends but a dismayed kind of surprise—a response that made Clair want to run and hide and never bother anyone again.

Clair tried smoothing the crinkle in her new suit. *Does it really matter?* Mist filled her eyes as she felt a twinge of envy—envy for the fierce kind of love that made family members protect one another. She'd never known such devotion intimately, but she knew she'd cherish the sentiment if it ever came her way.

How could she blame Leslie for shielding her dear brother from the likes of a nobody like her—someone who had no money and no connections. *No sense in lamenting my past. It does no good. Haven't you learned that yet?*

Clair released a long, moaning sigh, thinking of Glenn and how he'd come to her rescue at the Silver Moon. How did he always know when she needed help?

Clair shoved her hair out of her eyes. She secured the door as she thought about Mabel Sugar's offer to buy the shop. *But what would I do then? Where would I work?*

Suddenly, a familiar face appeared in the window—her old neighbor, Mrs. Plow. Clair unlocked the door and let her in.

"Hi there, missy. How are ya?" The old woman lumbered in, dressed in a lively colored poncho. "You like my getup?"

"Yes. You look like a rainbow." Clair also noticed Mrs. Plow had taken a bath.

The older woman grinned, showing her missing teeth. "Things ain't always as they seem, missy." She ambled around the shop like she already knew where everything was. "You glad to see me?"

"Yes, of course." Clair smiled. "Would you like to sit down? You look a little tired."

"Fiddlesticks." Mrs. Plow fingered a pink ceramic angel bell, which sat on top of a box of gift items. "Oh my. Looky here at this purdy thing." She shook it, causing it to make a tiny tickling sound. Then she rested the angel against her cheek. "Works on this old heart like a tonic." She did a little jig as if she were young again.

"Would you like to have it?"

"Ohh, ain't you sweet. I always knowed you were like your ma." Mrs. Plow clasped the angel in her hand and it disappeared under her poncho. "Course, you was always a sweet one." She smiled and a reminiscent look came over her. "Truth be told, I loved all the children in the neighborhood, even the ornery ones who got into my flowers, like that Glenny boy. But you was always my favorite."

Glenny?

"Yes'm, you was my favorite, for sure." The old woman limped over to Clair, reached up, and cradled her face in her gnarled hands. "Well, I best be saying my good-byes."

"Thank you for coming by."

The old woman sashayed toward the door. "I hear tell that Glenny Yves boy grew up right fine. Just goes to show you." The bell above the door jingled, and Mrs. Plow disappeared like the angel bell.

Clair gasped. What did she mean, Glenny Yves? A roar filled Clair's ears. *Glenn Yves is the boy I watched from the attic— the boy with flowers and letters and a promise to set me free.*

The room began to spin as she slumped to the floor unconscious.

nineteen

Clair drifted in and out of awareness. Someone's warm breath tickled her face. Had she been asleep at the bookshop? Had someone just kissed her? But who?

"Home," she heard herself say from a long distance. A familiar voice spoke to her, but it, too, sounded far away. Muffled somehow. Was Jesus calling her? *Am I dead?* She felt suspended in the air. "Hudson?" she whispered to anyone who could hear.

"It's Glenn. I've been worried about you. I almost called 911. I can still call for help."

Clair rubbed her forehead. "No." Her eyes focused, and then she realized Glenn was leaning over her. "I'll be all right. I just fainted. It's always been a weakness of mine." She felt silly causing such a fuss, although she did feel safe.

He looked into her eyes but said nothing.

"I'm all right now." She smiled.

Glenn didn't budge. "I think you should go to a doctor about this. Promise me you will, or I will take you to the emergency room."

"Okay."

He helped her up and into a soft chair.

Promise. She remembered that word from somewhere. The reality of Mrs. Plow's words came back to her. Glenn had promised to return to her when he'd grown up.

"Mrs. Plow was just here." She looked up into his eyes. "She told me. . ." Clair stopped cold, unsure of how much to reveal. Would it be best to let Glenn take the lead?

"Ah." Surprise lit up Glenn's face. "So. . .you know. . .who I am?"

Clair nodded but couldn't manage to say anything. Not yet.

"The ever-present Mrs. Plow. She used to shoo me out of her garden." He chuckled as he pulled up a chair next to her. "Guess I picked too many of her flowers that summer."

"Glenn Yves, so that's where you got all those flowers." She shook her head at him and smiled. "I remember you used to send them to me in a bundle along with a note. And you'd hooked it up to some kind of rope and pulley—"

"Which was attached to my tree house." Glenn grinned. "I was very resourceful."

"Yes, you were. I never did figure out how you attached that apparatus so near my attic window."

He gripped the arm of her chair. "So, you *do* remember me, then?"

"I do now. But you look so different, I didn't recognize you before."

"It's probably best. I was quite a gangly little kid, and my head was too—too big for my body." Glenn stuttered on his words a bit. "Well, some would say I've *still* got the bighead." He let out a snicker.

"Why didn't I see you at school? You moved again, didn't you?"

"Yes, we moved into your neighborhood at the beginning of the summer, and then we moved *out* of your neighborhood before the school year started. My family couldn't seem to stay put. So I never got to talk to you." Glenn folded his arms and looked at her intently. "And as I recall now, that turned out to be one of the disappointments of my youth."

Clair touched his arm. "I saved every one of your notes, but you never signed them. I never knew your name."

"I was trying to be mysterious. Guess it came off looking a little ridiculous."

"Not at all." She smiled. "I wanted to respond to your notes but never had the courage."

"I wish you had." He took her hand and gave it a squeeze.

Clair drew in a deep breath and offered him a beseeching expression. "The night at the party. . .did you have it all planned out to meet me?" She looked into his eyes. "It's okay. I just need to know. I could never be angry with you. You've helped me so much. I will forever be grateful to you."

"No, I can assure you, it was a God thing, nothing contrived. When I met you at the party that night, I had no idea who you were. I can honestly say I was drawn to you, though I couldn't explain why. When you disappeared so quickly, I was alarmed, and that's the only reason I came after you. Presumptuous, I know."

She offered him a weak smile. "But nice. Kind."

"It wasn't until the limo pulled up in front of your house that I realized. . .it had to be you." He shook his head. "At least, I hoped. . .prayed it was you."

Clair's mouth went dry. "Is that why you offered to help me, why you went to so much trouble for me? Was that your way of coming back for me like you said you would do in your note?" *But why do I need to know? What does it matter?* She licked her lips.

Glenn rose from his chair and slipped his hands in his pockets. "I never totally forgot about my last note to you, though I had tucked it away in the recesses of my mind." He sat back down and looked at her. "Then when the Lord brought us back together the night of the party, I thought of it as a gift. I started falling in love with you all over again. I felt as if it were a miracle. . .us meeting again the way we did."

She felt compelled to ask more. "So, there really was a Walter Sullivan who helped you?" *Did Glenn actually say he loved me? How can this be?*

"Yes, Walter is real. . .although he passed away years ago."

"I'm sorry to hear it." Clair took in a gulp of air. "But why didn't you tell me who you were?"

"I don't know." Glenn gave her a mirthless laugh. "Well, I guess I *do* know. I was always ashamed of my family's poverty. I found it humiliating." He wrinkled his brow. "As a kid, I felt as if I was born into my family by accident. I was a king in a jester's house. Pretty cocky, huh?" He shook his head. "Just like Drew said."

"I thought you were sweet. Those bundles of flowers you sent me were the only ones I've ever gotten." She squeezed his hand.

Before she drew away, Glenn covered her hand with his. "Oh, now that *is* appalling. I'm surprised men haven't showered you with roses." He tilted his head, looking regretful. "I'm sorry you found out this way. I intended to tell you soon. It's just. . .the time never seemed right." His expression grew more serious. "This stepfather you mentioned. . . Did he harm you?"

"No. But I guess you could say he hurt my heart. Children do have this intense need to be loved."

"Yes, they do. And rightly so." Glenn sighed. "And the attic? You weren't up there just for play, were you?"

"No."

"I wish I'd *done* something. . .told someone." Glenn's head drooped against his chest.

She knew he was grieving about her past. Without thinking, Clair took hold of his face and gently tilted his head to look at her. "I doubt anyone would have believed you anyway. My stepfather could be chameleon-like at times. And it's all over now. All is well. Okay?" In the silence, she could hear the clock in the back room chime away the hour.

"Okay." Glenn gazed into her eyes as if he were memorizing every nuance of her face. "I had intended to surprise you tonight. I wanted to make this moment romantic in every way. All the things you deserve—candlelight and violins. But I'm going to be selfish and just come out with it." He took in a deep breath. "I've fallen in love with you, Clair."

The words still sounded foreign to her, coming out of his mouth. Anyone's mouth. "How can this be?" What had Glenn said at the restaurant? *Sometimes the surprises of life will take us by storm.*

"You're stunned." He lifted her hand to his lips. "And I don't blame you."

Once again Clair felt lightheaded. *God, is this a sign?* Had she fallen in love with the wrong man? Then she recalled the promise in Glenn's final note. She understood now. He was just trying to fulfill a childhood vow. "The note. I would never hold you to it."

Glenn shook his head and his eyes grew misty. "What I've said today has nothing to do with that oath. I'm no longer a boy with childish notes and self-indulgent emotions. I'm a grown man, and these feelings couldn't be more real."

Clair felt his tenderness and sincerity all the way to her heart, and yet she felt a profound weight of confusion in her spirit. "You've been kind to me in so many ways, but. . ." Her voice left her.

"Yes?" Glenn kissed her hand as he gazed at her with a look of expectancy.

What were the right words? What would they be? Telling

Glenn the truth—that she didn't feel the same way—felt wrong to her, and yet returning his feelings seemed impossible.

Falling in love wasn't supposed to be mystifying like a puzzle with missing pieces. Was it?

A flicker of pain crossed his face. "You're in love with someone else?"

Clair lowered her gaze.

He let go of her hand. "Do you need some time to think about it?"

How could she break his heart? Glenn was a good Christian man. Clair faltered with uncertainty. She felt a displaced kind of ache, and she knew that feeling was connected to a man in a guitar shop only a few doors down. *How ungrateful you are, Clair. You want too much.*

She reached over and touched Glenn on the cheek. "You are so good to me. Maybe I just need a little time."

He looked away for a moment. "There is a party tonight. As your mentor, I would love to show you off." He smiled at her. "I mean, look at you. Beauty. Intelligence. Grace. You're amazing."

Clair wanted to disagree, but perhaps that approach wasn't as humble as it was impolite. "Thank you."

"But you know, you've always had all these gifts inside you. You just needed someone to help you unwrap them."

"And you did." She gripped the arm of the chair. "I so appreciate all you've done for me."

"Believe me, it was my pleasure," Glenn said. "So. . .will you go out with me tonight?"

Clair hesitated.

Silence fell between them. "What is it you want from life, Clair?" he whispered.

"Sometimes I don't know how to. . .just be. I guess that makes no sense."

Glenn cleared his throat. "You want to know what I think?"

"Yes, I do."

"You haven't given me the details about the attic, but I get this feeling your opinions and ambitions got locked away in there. A bird cannot take to the air in a cage." Glenn took hold of her hand again. "For instance, do you know what your favorite things are. . .like your favorite ice cream?"

"I don't know. I usually just eat chocolate or vanilla."

"One day you must remedy that. But maybe I should ask you this—what is the essence of Ms. O'Neal? What is it you'd do if nothing could stop you?"

"But I'm just Clair."

"No." He flinched. "You are indomitable."

"I know now I'm capable of more than I ever dreamed possible. But I still feel I can't choose whatever I like. We mortals do have some limitations." Clair grinned.

"I know that kind of thinking from personal experience, and you don't want to limit the Creator." He released her. "Don't let other people choose your path. Not even me."

"Would I be able to sing?" *Why did I let that slip out of my mouth?*

"You can sing?" He leaned back, looking astonished. "You never mentioned it before."

Clair winced, wishing she hadn't bought up the subject. "I love music."

"But why didn't you tell me this? I had no idea."

"I barely knew myself. You were right. I've hardly thought about my own life."

Glenn took a book from the shelf and stared at it as if it

were an adversary. "The shop. . .it was Ima's dream, wasn't it?"

"I cared for Ima. . .very much. So I thought I should do it because of love."

He slid the book back among the others. "That might seem like the honorable thing to do, but it will make for a miserable existence. . .living other people's lives for them. And you've had more than your share of unhappiness already."

"Yes." Clair felt such relief, knowing people dearest to her would allow her to release the bookshop into more capable hands—hands that were meant to take over for Ima. She looked back at Glenn, her heart aching with gratitude. "I owe you so much. I wish I could repay you."

Glenn turned the onyx ring on his finger and grinned at her. "Well, you could always tell me you've fallen in love with me, too. That would be a good start."

Clair squeezed his hand. *Lord, please give me courage.* "I wish I could. But God has other plans for us both." She leaned over and kissed him on the cheek. "I have a great fondness for you, but. . ."

"Yes." Glenn held up his hand. "I understand. I do." He looked down at the floor. "You shouldn't go with me tonight. It wouldn't be fair to either of us." After a long pause, he rose. "Well then. . ." He slid his hands into his pockets and walked to the door.

Clair followed him. When he stopped at the door, she physically turned him back around to face her. "But to be loved and cared for in any way—even like a brother—is a good thing. Isn't it?"

"Yes." He held her gently by the shoulders. "Love is always good, always welcome."

"And you not only kept the promise you made to Walter, you kept *your* promise to me."

"I did?"

"Yes, you also said someday when you were grown, you'd come back to set me free." Tears stung her eyes. "And you did, Glenn Yves. The Lord used you to set me free."

He touched her cheek. "Set you free. . .to love another."

She wished she could take the sadness from his eyes. Oh, how she cared for him—like the brother she never had. She reached up and hugged him. "I will always remember you, always think kindly of you wherever you are." Tears filled her eyes.

Glenn pulled out a handkerchief from his pocket and wiped away the tears now spilling down her face. "Promise?"

Smiling back at him, she grasped the lapels of his jacket. "Yes. I promise."

twenty

Once Glenn crossed the street, Clair bolted the door and sat back down on the chair to absorb what had happened. Suddenly all the good things in her new life seemed to have vanished.

I said no to a marriage with a fine Christian man. I've chosen to run away from Ima's dream. I will move from the only home I've ever known to live in an apartment. And I will never be able to marry the man I truly love.

All seemed utterly lost or, at best, misplaced. Nothing remained, except a bit more confidence. She rarely chewed on her lip or twisted her clothes anymore when she got nervous. Her shoulders were straight and her outfit fashionable. But without love and a home, what did she really have left?

Clair smelled the lingering scent of his cologne in the air. *Glenn Yves.* She thought of his kindness to her in their youth, the way he'd grasped her hand with such affection and his grave countenance when she'd refused him. How could she deny him? Maybe she could go to the party after all and tell him she'd changed her mind.

But what can I really give Glenn? Were affection and fondness enough to last a lifetime? She knew the truth: Glenn deserved to be loved as deeply as she loved Hudson.

Love. She couldn't escape that word. She loved Hudson, and she loved him in the marrying way. There was no turning back from those feelings, but they were sentiments she could never take pleasure in.

Just as Clair had always done in the midst of life's sorrows, she started singing one of her favorite songs. This time, it was "Amazing Grace." When she finished, an idea came to her—Hudson had not been allowed to make one of the most important decisions of his life. And the flash of pain she'd seen in his eyes as she left the café with Glenn had been almost unbearable. No doubt she'd caused Hudson great pain, but Clair had become so convinced the decision would help him in the end she'd been blinded to the facts. Wasn't Hudson old enough and wise enough to choose his own way?

What a fool I've been. What have I thrown away? Like the settling of cement, resolution hardened in her mind. She would make things right again. *And I won't waste another minute.*

A familiar-looking woman in a purple hat jiggled the door handle and then pattered lightly on the glass. "Yoo-hoo. Mabel Sugar here."

Clair let her inside. "I'm glad to see you, Mabel."

"Oh, it's good to see you again, honey." The older woman looked over her reading glasses at Clair. "Have you had a chat with the good Lord about my offer?"

She didn't want to hurry Mabel out the store, but Clair felt determined to see Hudson right away. "I have," she started, "but unfortunately, I have some personal business to attend to right now. Could you meet me tomorrow around noon? We can discuss the sale of the bookshop." She almost wished Glenn could see her now.

"Thank you, Jesus." Mabel gave her hand a little wave in the air. "I would not only love to meet you, I will treat you to lunch. Do you like the River Grill?"

Clair smiled as she answered. "Yes, that sounds wonderful."

"You've got it. Lunch tomorrow. Noon at the River Grill.

I'll see you then." Mabel smiled broadly and exited, humming a gospel tune.

Clair waited for Mabel to cross the street, and then she quickly locked up and strode toward Hudson's guitar shop. Her only fear was that he'd changed his mind—that he'd given up on her.

As she stepped into the guitar shop, she breathed in Hudson's world. A wide assortment of electric and acoustic guitars hung on the walls and a checkout counter stood in the middle of the big room. There were rows and rows of sheet music and books on the how-tos of playing the guitar, and someone could be heard strumming an electric guitar in the back. *Students, maybe? I can't believe I've never been in this store before.*

A young man at the counter, who'd been watching her, suddenly hollered, "Yo, over there. Something I can do for you?"

"Yes." She strode over to him. "I would like to speak with Hudson Mandel, please." Clair gripped the handle on her purse until her fingers throbbed.

He made an open-palm gesture with his hands. "Oh, sorry. Just missed him."

"Really?"

"He left for a wedding." He leaned on the counter, looking at her a little bug-eyed.

"A wedding? Surely not his own." Clair's heart skipped a beat.

"No. One of his friends is getting married today."

Clair sighed audibly.

"You one of his friends?"

"I hope so. I'm Clair."

"Ohh. Are you *the* Clair?" He flipped his long hair behind his shoulder. "From the song?"

"Yes."

"Awesome. It's really cool to meet you. We were beginning to think you were a figment of Hudson's imagination."

She reached out to shake his hand. "Clair O'Neal."

"Leroy Goldstein." He shook her hand like a water pump. "Yeah, awesome." His head angled like he was mulling something over. "Listen, Hudson got there really early for a sound check, so if you want to stop by, it'd be a good move. Grace Cathedral. It's not far from the capitol building."

"Yes, I know where it is." Clair headed toward the door. "Thank you. . .very much."

"All right." He lifted his arms in a gesture of victory. "You go for it!"

Clair strode out of the shop toward her car. How many minutes would it take to get there—how long to make things right? Her stride broke into a run.

Once she'd arrived at the church and scurried up the steps, she halted at the double white doors. How would she explain her recent behavior without turning Hudson against his sister? She paused for a moment to give herself time to think. Clouds of what-ifs and warnings entered her mind like swarming bees, but this time she tried not to listen. Instead, she pulled open the door and eased herself inside.

She stood in the foyer, which appeared empty and silent. Deathly quiet, in fact. *Where is everyone?* Had she gone to the wrong church? She slipped off down a side hallway, in search of Hudson.

Just then a door burst open at the far end of the hallway. Girls and young women and older ladies dressed in pastel finery all burst out of the room as if there were a fire. The last woman to emerge was adorned in heaps of white satin and tulle. The ladies formed a hugging, laughing gauntlet for the beaming bride. Clair stepped out of their way.

The bride stopped in front of Clair. "You seem lost, hon."

"I'm looking for someone."

"Maybe I can help." The other ladies bustled on their way as the bride took hold of Clair's arm. "Walk with me."

They strolled down a hallway as the bride's luscious gown swished alongside of Clair. *What a lovely sound.*

"Now who are you looking for, hon?"

"Hudson Mandel."

"Why, he's one of my husband's friends. He's playing at our wedding." The bride took a good, long look at her. "Ohh, you must be Clair. I'm so glad you could make it. Last time I asked Hudson, he didn't think you'd be coming. By the way, I'm Susanna Cartwright." She gave Clair a hug. "Well, I'll be a Cartwright for a few more minutes anyway." The bride-to-be wiggled her eyebrows.

Clair chuckled, feeling overjoyed Hudson would mention her to his closest friends.

"Let's go this way." Susanna led Clair through another maze of hallways until they reached a door that led into the main sanctuary. She pointed through the doorway to the stage. "There's your man."

Clair blushed.

"There's plenty of time before the guests start arriving. Now go after him." Susanna winked.

"By the way, I hope you have a wonderful marriage."

"Oh, I'm sure we'll see each other again. But thanks." Susanna gently nudged Clair forward and then swished away in her bridal gown like a swan taking off from a lake.

Clair eased her way into the sanctuary and gasped. The church overflowed with yellow roses and ivory candles. *Oh my.* Then her eyes searched out Hudson. There he stood—

hooking up his guitar to an amp. She watched him for a moment. A familiar voice in her head told her she didn't belong. *No, that's not true. I belong with Hudson.* She took a tentative step forward.

Hudson turned toward her as if he sensed her presence. "Clair." He almost lost the grip on his guitar. "Why. . .what are you doing here?"

She swallowed hard. Hudson wore a light gray tuxedo and looked more handsome than ever. *I hope he's happy to see me.* She circled her arms around her middle for comfort. "I came. . . to talk."

"I'm just really surprised to see you." He set his guitar on a stand and strode over to her.

"I know this isn't the best time to say this, but—"

"No, this is the perfect time," Hudson said.

"I don't really want to say good-bye." She moved a little closer to him. "If that's okay."

Hudson let out a deep sigh. "Oh, that's more than okay."

"I want to start where we left off at the park."

"I think that can be arranged."

Longing filled his eyes, and another sharp pain of remorse coursed through her. *How could I have hurt him so?* Between the intoxicating aroma of roses and Hudson's nearness, she felt she might do something a little impetuous. "And I want to begin right here." She kissed her fingers and then reached over to softly touch his lips.

Clair could feel his breath on her hand as its ebb and flow increased. She placed her hand on the back of his neck, drew him to her, and kissed him full on the lips. Her fingers gently tugged on his hair as she intensified the kiss. When she felt satisfied Hudson had a keen understanding of her regret in leaving, she drew back.

He tried to catch his breath. "Whoa. Do you think you could leave me and come back again?"

Laughing, Clair tried to calm herself as well. She wasn't used to being so forward. . .or so happy.

Applause and whistles exploded near them, startling them both. They glanced around, looking for the ruckus. To the side, the bridal party, including the bride herself, clapped and grinned with gusto.

"You go, girl!" Susanna hollered.

For once, the only heat on Clair's face was the warmth left by their kiss. She nodded and smiled at Susanna.

When the commotion and laughter settled down, Hudson turned to Clair. "Tell me, what changed your mind?"

Clair had known that question would come, but she still hadn't figured out an honest reply that wouldn't incriminate his sister.

"I think I know." Hudson frowned. "I called Leslie right before I came here, and she sounded unusually guilty. Please tell me, has my sister been playing in the wrong sandbox?"

twenty-one

Clair opened her mouth, but nothing came out.

"So, it's true," Hudson said. *Leslie's out of control again.*

"Your sister was only watching out for you." Clair squeezed his arm. "She loves you."

Hudson couldn't think clearly when Clair stood so near. He took in a deep breath. "Okay. What did my sister do *exactly*?" He found himself gripping his guitar pick until it hurt his palm. "I can tell you don't want to say anything, but this has been going on too long. And it stops here." He took hold of Clair's hand. "Please, before the guests start arriving, we need to talk. In fact, will you be my date for the wedding?"

She touched the jacket on her silvery gray suit. "Am I dressed okay?"

"Yes, you certainly are." He leaned toward her, kissing her lightly on the cheek. "There's something else you need to know about my sister." Hudson cleared his throat. "Let's sit for a minute."

After they'd settled themselves down on a front pew, he said, "You know, I'd do anything for Leslie. We Mandels stick up for each other. Always have, but. . ."

"Yes?"

"I can't let her go on manipulating my life." Hudson leaned forward, resting on his knees. "It all started when our mother got sick. I was a kid then, and Leslie was ten years older. Mom put her in charge of me for a while." He looked back at Clair. "Actually, I have to give Leslie credit. She did a pretty good job helping out. But I'm a grown man now, and she keeps forgetting that."

"I can't imagine having a sibling who cares so much."

He thought of Clair's lonely youth and realized she might not understand older sisters who could be overbearing at times. He leaned back gazing at her. The look in her eyes could stop a raging battle and warm the coldest heart. "Yes, but—"

"Mr. Mandel!" someone hollered from behind them. "Ready for a sound check."

Hudson groaned. "Excuse me again," he said to Clair. "I guess this isn't the best time for an intimate talk."

She touched his hand. "Are you sure I should be at this wedding?"

Hudson leaned over and brushed her cheek with a kiss. "I am *very* sure."

≈

After the ceremony, the guests flooded toward the reception, which was being held in a conservatory-like room adjoining the church. Hudson held hands with Clair as they maneuvered through the crowd.

"I've never seen a room like this before," Clair whispered as if in awe. "A glass ceiling and growing orchids and a piano in the middle of it all."

"The church uses it for all kinds of functions. Sometimes they have weddings in here as well."

She looked around. "It's so enchanting."

He loved watching Clair; she was always so full of wonder and innocence.

Then, as if too much bliss could bring some kind of wrath down on them both, he saw a sight he'd been dreading. His sister and Tara Williamson were walking toward them from across the room at an alarming pace, and the look on Leslie's face wasn't one of merriment. He'd always hated confrontation. *But I will make my position clear to them. Right now.*

Leslie approached them first, wearing a bizarre pink feathery garment. Hudson couldn't help but notice that, with her skinny legs, his sister looked just like a flamingo.

"Well, *there* you are," Leslie crooned with a slight edge in her voice.

"You were wonderful," Tara said to Hudson.

"Clair." Leslie's eyes grew wide "I love your outfit. Another gift from Glenn?"

Hudson's eye began to twitch. He mashed his finger against his eyelid to stop the spasm. The pianist started playing something cheerful, but he was no longer in a festive mood. "Leslie?"

"Yes?" Leslie batted her eyelashes with a comical air.

"May I see you in private?" Not waiting for his sister to respond, he took hold of her arm. "Please excuse us," he said to Clair and Tara. "We'll be back in a minute." Hudson then shepherded Leslie off to a private corner.

"How dare you herd me over here like a toddler? What's this all about?" Leslie jerked her arm free.

"You are a good woman. But what has made you into this ever-circling vulture looking for innocent blood?" Hudson rebuked himself, wishing he'd used a little more finesse with his language. "I'm sorry. That was my anger talking. But you know what I'm referring to—the game you're playing at Clair's expense." He crossed his arms for effect. "And when Clair refused to go out with me, I had no idea it was your fault."

"*Moi?*" Leslie shrank back with her hand over her throat.

"I'm thirty-one years old. I know when you're lying. You

get this twittering thing going in your jaw."

"Twittering? Great word. I'll have to use it somewhere."

Hudson shook his head. "You know, Leslie, you were a great help to Mom all those years ago when she needed you. You were terrific, in fact. But don't spoil those incredibly selfless acts by continuing to pretend I'm a child. I know you think my life would be perfect with Tara, but—"

"It would be."

"How can you say that?" Hudson looked at her incredulously.

"Because I know you better than anyone else does."

"Obviously not." He shook his head in disbelief. "If you really knew me, you would know that I would never be interested in a marriage without love. I like Tara. I like her a lot. But I *love* Clair, and I'm praying she'll marry me someday. So, you have a choice here. You can continue to push Clair away. . .and make me miserable. Or you can trust me to make a wise choice about my own life and be happy for us."

"Well. . ."

"You know, if you'd love having Tara for a sister-in-law so much, then maybe you could marry Tara's brother, Jerold. His praise of you is inexhaustible."

Leslie suddenly looked lost in thought. "Is that true about Jerold?"

Hudson nodded.

"Hmm." Leslie's frown melted like butter.

"Come on now." Hudson smiled, hoping to make the most of the mellow moment. "You'll love Clair once you get to know her."

Leslie shifted her weight, balancing her stiletto heel on the marble floor. "You're incredibly talented, and I just want the best for you."

How can I get through to her? Leslie is so much better than this. "Clair *is* God's best for me. I've never been more sure of anything in my life."

Leslie arched an eyebrow.

"Your opinion has always mattered so much to me," Hudson continued. "And you've been there for me every step of the way. That's why it's so important to me now that you see God's hand in this."

She gave him a pensive stare.

Hudson opted for a different approach. "Look, your novels are full of characters who are courageous and noble. People love your characters. *I* love your characters."

"You do?"

"Of course I do." He lowered his voice but remained firm. "But we need a little heroism off the pages, sis."

Leslie clicked her tongue. "Well, I guess my little brother has finally grown up."

"He did a long time ago. You just needed to acknowledge it."

"Okay, okay." Leslie raised her hands in mock defeat. "I'll try. I really will." She patted Hudson's cheek, and with a cheerless expression, sauntered toward the piano.

Hudson turned and bumped into Tara as she came around the corner. "Tara?" He pulled back in surprise. Had she been standing on the other side of the wall, listening to them? "So, how much of that did you just hear?"

Tara flipped her dark hair back. Even though she looked nonchalant, there were tears in her eyes. "I heard most of it. But the only words I remember are, 'I like Tara, but I love Clair.'"

twenty-two

Hudson realized the time had come to put an end to Tara's misguided hopes. "You know, it's been some time since we dated."

"I know." Tara smoothed her already perfect suit.

"I thought you'd moved on," Hudson said gently. "Weren't you dating Peter McKinney from church?" Tara's heavy perfume made him take a step backward.

"It's been over for a while." Her mouth curved up on one side. "I found out no one else was quite like Hudson Mandel." She glanced in a mirror nearby and adjusted her strands of pearls. "And well, I'm not used to being cast off."

"We both agreed to stop dating. No one was cast off."

"Well, I've had second thoughts about our agreement. But I guess you haven't." Tara nodded in Clair's direction. "You've moved on quite well, I see."

"I'm truly sorry for any pain I've caused you."

"Oh, I'll recover." Tara smirked. "I come from a long line of survivors. And I've discovered something—my daddy's money really does soften the blows of life."

Hudson had no idea what to say, so he decided to let her talk it out. He just hoped Clair didn't mind waiting a bit longer.

"I'll go on a singles' cruise around the Greek isles. Should take the last little sting out of things." Tara sauntered away and then suddenly turned back with a forlorn expression. "I will miss the music, though. I loved your music. And you don't look too bad in that tux, either." She blew him a kiss and, without looking back again, strode swiftly out the door.

Hudson wondered how he could have ever found Tara interesting enough to date. What had been the attraction? She was stunning but way too smug. Surely he hadn't been small-minded enough to date her just for her looks. Or had the career promises from Tara's family caused him to hang around a little longer than he should have? He searched his heart, hoping he wouldn't find anything too devious or shallow.

As he continued to muse over his past, Hudson glanced around, hoping to find Clair. He strode back to the section of the conservatory where he'd left her, but she wasn't there. Had Clair driven home? *How can I blame her?* He'd convinced her to stay as his guest and then he promptly abandoned her.

Hudson turned toward the piano and saw the most amazing sight; Clair stood on the other side of the conservatory, having a lively chat with several people. He observed her for a moment. She had all the same wonderful qualities as when he'd first met her, but she had more confidence. Then he remembered Glenn Yves, who'd mentored her. Even though Glenn may have been competition for Clair's affections, he'd made a genuine difference in her life. *What can I give her but my love?*

Suddenly Clair's gaze met his from across the room, and he felt a rush of joy.

She waved without appearing upset in the least.

Hudson made his way around the clusters of guests to join her. Clair circled her arm through his, and they strolled toward the bride and groom.

"Is everything okay?" Clair asked.

"Yes." Hudson covered her hand with his. "I'm sorry about that scene back there. It was rude and totally uncalled for."

"I'm all right." Her smile looked a little anxious. "But I

don't want to hurt your relationship with your sister—"

"First of all, no matter what the enticement, I don't want to marry Tara. And Leslie. . .well, she'll come around. Once she decides it's her idea for us to be together, then you won't find a more loyal subject."

Clair seemed to study his face, and then she leaned her head against him. "I've always wanted a sister."

Hudson kissed her forehead, taking pleasure in the softness of her skin.

A burst of laughter drew their attention to the newly married couple. Susanna and Brad were giggling and feeding each other hunks of the wedding cake as cameras flashed all around them. Every movement they made together looked like a snapshot.

Hudson silently rejoiced with his friends and then wondered how Clair would respond to a proposal of marriage. "We're having a family get-together at my parents' house tomorrow evening. If you came with me. . .well, it would be a great way for me to introduce you to my family. And it would give Leslie a chance to get to know you better."

Clair took in a deep breath. "Yes, I would love to go."

"Good."

"Do you think your parents will like me?" Concern shadowed her lovely face.

Hudson put his hand on the small of her back. "They will adore you. As you know, Leslie has issues, but some of it is because she's eccentric. You know. . .writers." He rolled his eyes, grinning. "The rest of my family is normal."

"Hey," Leslie said, appearing at his side, "I heard that."

He reached over and gave his sister a peck on the cheek. Within days, he predicted, she and Clair would be the best of friends.

twenty-three

Clair slipped on one of her new dresses—a luscious ice pink linen. Hopefully, it would help make a good first impression on Hudson's parents.

As she stared in the mirror, she also saw the other gift Glenn had left her—a sureness in her stance. In fact, sometimes when she saw her reflection, she still had trouble recognizing herself.

Just as she turned her attention to her shoes, the doorbell rang. *Hudson?* She looked at a clock. *Too early. Maybe it's the Realtor.* She trotted to the front door and opened it. "Glenn?"

"Hi, Clair."

Glenn brightened her doorway with his one-of-a-kind smile—the same one he'd worn the evening she'd first met him. But surprisingly, he was dressed casually in jeans, a pullover, and loafers.

He whistled. "You look spectacular in that dress, like a string of pink diamonds."

"Thank you." She wanted Glenn to feel welcome, but she wondered what Hudson might think of his presence.

Glenn looked around. "I just came by to tell you something. I'm moving to LA."

"Really? Why?" Clair wondered if declining his proposal had anything to do with his move.

"I need a change. I have some friends out there. And, well, I shouldn't have any trouble finding work as an image coach in LA. Although, I did have plenty of work here, it's just. . ."

His voice trailed off.

Clair could see the sadness in his eyes, even though she knew he tried to hide it.

"Listen, I know it didn't work out for us. But I hope. . ." Glenn choked on his words. "But I hope we can always be friends."

"Always." Mist filled Clair's eyes. "You changed my life in such a good way. Walter Sullivan would be proud of you."

Glenn chuckled. "Yeah. If he could see you, he'd be proud of us both."

"Thank you." Should she tell him she was indeed selling the shop and her home? The time didn't seem right.

Glenn looked across the street. "This neighborhood. . .it's kind of surreal standing here. Brings back a lot of memories for me. Good and bad."

"I wish you and your family had never moved away. I would've liked to have had a friend."

"You did. And you still do." Glenn smiled. "I just want you to promise me. . .if you ever need help of any kind that you won't hesitate to call. I won't be too hard to find."

"Okay." Clair chewed on her lower lip.

"Well, I *almost* broke you of that habit." He gestured to her lips.

She chuckled.

He tilted his head, looking at her with eyes full of emotion. "You say your life's been changed. But you're not the only one." He lowered his gaze. "You showed me the right kind of love, the real thing, is possible. And I'm glad to know it." He looked back at her, clasping his hands tightly and then letting them drop to his side.

To her, Glenn looked like a boy again, timid and restless, and her heart nearly broke.

"Well, good-bye, sweet Clair." He turned to go.

" 'Bye," she whispered. She reached out and hugged him. "I will miss you."

Glenn held her for a moment. He touched her chin and then released her. "Would you like to know one of my regrets as a kid?"

"Yes?"

"I wish I'd sent more flowers to a girl named Clair O'Neal. You know, with my little rope from the tree house."

Clair grew serious. "You made me feel less alone that summer. And it meant more to me than you'll ever know."

"Thanks." Glenn smiled. "Well then." He bowed slightly and then walked toward his car.

She waved good-bye to Glenn as he drove away, but moments later, the tears began to flow. She clutched her heart. *He loved me, and I could not love him back.*

After a long cry and an even longer prayer for Glenn, Clair cleaned up her face in the bathroom. She'd done the only thing she could think of—release him into the loving hands of the Almighty and pray that God would bless him in every way imaginable. . .especially in love.

The doorbell came to life again. *Hudson?* But when Clair opened the door, she saw an Indian gentleman on her steps holding a peach-colored urn filled with a zillion kinds of flowers. A bee followed the man, buzzing around his head.

"These are for you, miss."

"They're so lovely."

"Oh yes, but I am wishing the bee did not think so, too," the man said in a lyrical Indian accent.

Clair chuckled, wondering who would have sent them. Hudson? Glenn?

The man waited for the bee to fly away and then placed

the huge bouquet in her hands.

She placed the flowers on the entry table and then handed him a tip. "Thank you so much."

"Oh yes. You are very welcome. I hope these flowers bring you much pleasure. It is what we endeavor to do," he said and then bustled off toward his floral van.

Clair stood over the enormous bouquet, breathing in the heady fragrance and sighing softly to herself. Except for the ones Glenn had given her from Mrs. Plow's garden, it was the first time anyone had given her flowers. *I've certainly had a lot of "firsts" lately.* The card simply read, "Lovingly, Hudson."

Just as Clair pushed on the door to close it, she saw Hudson coming up the walk. Her heart's tempo picked up a few extra beats. "Hello."

Hudson stopped at the door. "Hi."

Thinking it was time she gave away some compliments instead of just collecting them, Clair said, "You look very handsome in those khakis and that blue silk shirt."

"Thank you." He grinned, leaning closer to her. "And you look lovely."

She reached over and kissed his cheek. "I got your flowers just now. They're so pretty."

"I have to be honest, sending you the flowers was someone else's idea."

She wondered what he meant. "Whose idea was it?"

"I got this anonymous note left at the Silver Moon Café. It read, 'Clair should never be without flowers.'"

She knew instantly who'd written the note. Glenn. If he couldn't buy them for her now, he'd make sure Hudson did. Mist stung her eyes.

Hudson smiled but looked uncomfortable. "Glenn sent the

note about the flowers?"

Clair slowly nodded.

"He fell in love with you." Hudson said it as a statement and not a question.

"Yes, he did." Perhaps Hudson had known all along.

"Hard to blame him. You're very easy to fall in love with."

What did Hudson mean? Maybe she should explain a bit more about Glenn. "He was my neighbor when I was a little girl. I mentioned that neighborhood boy to you, but at the time I didn't know it was Glenn Yves. It was quite a surprise when I found out. As you know, he'd been kind to me during some rough times growing up."

"So Glenn turned out to be the neighbor kid you talked about. Amazing." Hudson touched her arm. "I must thank him someday. . .for all his help."

Clair looked at him. "Glenn came by to tell me he's moving to LA."

"I wish him well." Hudson looked at her with a tender expression. "But do you mind if I ask what your feelings were for him?"

She breathed a quick prayer for the right words. "I'm grateful for his help, and I'm very fond of him. . .like a brother."

Hudson let out a puff of air and raked his fingers through his hair. "Well, I guess you should know that makes me feels good"—he rested his hand over his heart—"right here."

"I'm glad." She reached up and stroked his cheek with her fingertips.

He grasped her hand and kissed it.

Clair wasn't sure how long they stood there, looking into each other's eyes, but time didn't seem to matter. At all. She wondered if she should tell him she'd accepted an offer on the house and about Mabel and the shop, but somehow all her news seemed unimportant at the moment.

A short ride later, they sat in front of Hudson's boyhood home. Clair took in the loveliness of it—a two-story Victorian house painted blue with dainty shutters and a white picket fence. "It's so quaint and pretty."

Hudson leaned forward, staring at the house. "My mom loves all things Victorian. I guess you can tell." He looked at her. "Are you still anxious about meeting my family?"

"I'll be fine." *The old Clair is gone. God, help me to remember.*

"It's okay if you're scared. If *your* parents were still alive, I'd be terrified."

Clair laughed. "Really?"

"Oh yeah. Listen, maybe it would help if you knew a few things about them. My dad loves golf and building furniture. He's hard of hearing, so he winces a lot when he's trying to hear you. My mother likes gardening and reading, but mostly she likes mothering, so she'll immediately take you under her wing until you feel completely smothered with attention."

"It all sounds. . .wonderful."

"Then you're at the right place." Hudson's eyebrows creased. "And then there's Leslie. What can I say, except somehow I think it'll be all right." He pointed toward the house. "Speaking of family. . ."

A middle-aged woman, wearing a dress in robin's-egg blue, came toward them. Clair opened her car door.

"Ohh, you must be Clair," the woman said, reaching to take her hand.

Hudson hurried around to Clair and helped her down from the pickup seat. He made some introductions, but Mrs. Mandel had already pulled Clair into a warm embrace.

"I've heard so much about you. I'm so glad you're here.

Come right on in. I've made some chicken and dumplings. . . from scratch. . .and some cherry cobbler. Edwin, Hudson's father, just loves it when I have company because he gets everything homemade."

Clair allowed the older woman to circle her arm through hers as they walked up the path to the house. She noticed Mrs. Mandel had a soft touch, smiled a great deal, and smelled of fresh dill.

Soon Clair was whisked into a world of warmth and beauty. She glanced around, taking note of the touches of blue in the pictures and the pillows and the circular rugs. To the right was a large living area with a stone fireplace, and to the left, a long oak table in the dining room. She wondered if Hudson's father had made it. A cuckoo clock went off somewhere in the house. There were homey touches all around her that spoke of cozy times with the family. *What must it be like?*

As introductions were made, Hudson's father shook her hand vigorously, and then Clair was escorted into the kitchen, where a myriad of homemade smells filled the air. She drank in the moment. "You've made such a lovely place to live. And I like all the blue."

"You do? Eddie thinks I've gone a little overboard," she said loudly. But—"

"Overboard is right. She dresses me in blue, too." Edwin grinned at Clair as he handed her a steaming cup of coffee.

Just as Clair thought she'd arrived in paradise, Leslie appeared in the doorway like a long, dark shadow. *You prepare a table before me in the presence of my enemies.* Clair stared at her and offered up a smile. *Dear Lord, please help me. What should I say?* She started with the obvious. "Hi."

Everyone turned toward Leslie. All bustle in the kitchen

stopped, and for a brief moment they all seemed suspended in time. Did they know about Leslie's attempts to be rid of her? *Are they waiting for my reaction?*

Before Leslie could utter a word, her mother smothered her with kisses and hugs.

Leslie melted into grins. "Okay." She pulled away and held up her hands in a pretend tragic posture. "All right. The desperado has died. The real Leslie you all adore is back." She stuffed her fingers through the loops of her lizard green slacks.

Family cheers broke out, leaving Clair stunned and silent. *What does this mean?*

Hudson slapped his sister on the back, and then Leslie gave him a good-humored slug.

Clair felt helpless, watching the spectacle. Was that the way families operated? Could problems turn into amusement as easily as ice melted into water? She took a sip of her coffee.

"I'm afraid I've behaved rather badly," Leslie said to Clair. "Like my heroine, Marionette, in *The Bush Master*, too intensely possessive. . .to the point of losing her good sense."

Mrs. Mandel looked at her daughter with a pensive air. "Yes, but Marionette had many good qualities, too." She kissed Leslie's cheek.

"I read *The Bush Master*," Clair said, deciding to go with the family flow. "I loved Marionette. It was hard not to admire the passionate concern she had for her family."

"Mmm. Please tell me more," Leslie said.

Clair's fingers tightened on the cup handle. "In the end, you could forgive Marionette for everything because you would want to know that kind of love."

"You're quite clever. . .the best subtextual dialogue I've ever heard." Leslie chuckled, leaning on the counter. "So, you liked *The Bush Master*?"

"Very much," Clair said. "I've read *all* your books."

"Really." Leslie slid a plate of chocolate biscotti in front of Clair. "Mmm. Might be nice to have a fan around. No one else in the family is."

An uproar arose, each one announcing in his or her own way that Leslie couldn't be more wrong.

Clair laughed, taking in the scene before her. She wondered what they would think if they knew this was her first encounter within a real family.

Leslie picked up a piece of biscotti. "And I've never seen Hudson as happy as when he's talking about you, Clair. I got to thinking. . .that has to be worth a lot."

"It's beyond price," Edwin said. "And it's still the way I feel about your mother after forty-one years."

A warm feeling spread through Clair. Perhaps she'd finally come home—a place she'd imagined hundreds of times but had never known. . .until now.

After the hoopla died down, Hudson ushered her out onto the back porch, which was lined with large glass windows and soft couches in a wide assortment of blues. "Ahh." He shut the door. "Alone at last."

Clair looked out over the huge backyard, which contained a garden complete with a waterfall and a wooden bridge. A pathway of gray stone meandered through flower beds frothing with daffodils and pink tulips. "Oh, your mother must love this garden."

"Yes." Hudson moved a few steps nearer to her, his voice deepening. "I believe she does."

He'd come so close, she could smell his cologne. *Mmm. Just like the outdoors.* But in spite of the romantic moment, she felt a sudden need to tell him about the bookshop. "I had lunch with a woman named Mabel. She wants to buy the shop. Has always wanted to buy it, actually."

Hudson sat down on a wicker chair near her. "I'm glad, since I think your heart wasn't really in it." He looked up at her with an earnest expression.

"This woman, Mabel, seems perfect. She came out of nowhere one day. It's like I was waiting for her." Clair sat next to him. "I've decided to sell it to her at a reasonable price. I think Ima would be pleased someone so capable and devoted would be running her store."

"And do you know what you want to do now?"

"Yes, I *do* know." Clair took in some extra oxygen and decided, sink or swim, to make the boldest announcement of her life. "I want to sing. . .with you."

twenty-four

Hudson's mouth dropped open.

Clair panicked, thinking she'd been too hasty in making such a presumptuous request. *Maybe I should tell him I plan to find another job as well.* "That is—"

"That is just what I've been praying for." He gathered her hands in his and kissed them. "There is nothing that would make me happier."

Relief filled Clair at his response, but she couldn't help but wonder how the decision would affect the future. Their future.

Hudson looked out at the garden. "Let's take a walk." He guided her from the back porch into the warm air of spring.

They ambled through the winding paths. The sound of ducks could be heard somewhere on the grounds. Finally they came to the middle of the little bridge, and Hudson turned around to face Clair. "My parents call this the kissing bridge."

Clair slid her hand along the smooth redwood railing, hoping Hudson would take full advantage of the bridge's nickname.

"I've been waiting for just the right moment. I hope this is it." Hudson looked at her as if he were collecting his thoughts. Then he pulled a small box out of his pocket and knelt on one knee.

Clair felt like she was dreaming. Could this really be happening?

"I have fallen so in love with you." Hudson's face shone with tenderness and affection. "Clair, I promise to cherish you all the days of my life." The velvet box crackled open, revealing a marquise diamond ring.

Clair's hand went to her heart. "You're asking me to marry you?"

"Yes. I believe I am."

Her eyes filled with tears. She wasn't prepared for the wild mixture of emotions inside her—gratitude, elation, and a fear she might wake up. "I'll say yes quickly just in case this is a dream."

Hudson rose and slipped the ring onto her finger.

"It's so lovely. This can't be happening. . .to me."

He placed his hands on her shoulders. "This is no dream." He pulled her into an embrace. "When I hold you. . .it's like you were always meant to be here."

She eased away and traced the contours of his face with her finger, lingering on his cheek. "This is all such a gift."

Hudson closed his eyes and kissed her tenderly on the forehead. "I accept this gift, Lord, in thankful awe." He then cupped her face with his hands, and with mist-filled eyes, he leaned down to kiss her.

Clair returned his sweet affections. *No more dark corners. Only light and love.* She laced her fingers around his as her heart overflowed with joy. Home at last.

❦

Three weeks later, Clair and Hudson held hands as they mounted the stairs inside the Silver Moon Café. Clair knew she was not only walking up to the stage, but to a new life in so many ways. She felt an excitement in the air—an electric sort of anticipation for what would soon come. She could hardly believe it. *I'm about to sing with my fiancé!* She glanced at the room full of people and at Hudson's family, including Leslie, all seated around a table, looking animated and happy.

"You're not nervous, are you?" Hudson whispered in her ear.

"Should I be?" She mirrored his smile.

He shook his head. "No, not at all."

Clair had wondered, in fact, over the past weeks why she hadn't been anxious about her first appearance, but she decided to count that stillness deep inside as one of God's mercies to her. She'd lost so much over the years, surely now was a time of restoration.

Clair knew she'd have no problem recalling her part of the song. Over the past three weeks, they'd practiced "The Love Song" to perfection—a song Hudson had written for their upcoming wedding.

Once they were on stage, they reluctantly let go of each other's hands. Not used to the spotlight, Clair winced a bit as her eyes got used to the brightness.

Hudson adjusted a microphone for Clair, pulled out a guitar pick from his pocket, and sat down on his wooden stool. "Good evening. I'm Hudson Mandel."

His fans rewarded him with an enthusiastic round of applause. "And I'd like to introduce Clair O'Neal. . .a new voice in Little Rock. Someone I think you're going to like. I'm also happy to say, she's my fiancée." Cheers went up all over the hall.

Clair could feel her face getting warm, but she didn't mind. She smiled at Hudson. His announcement felt good all the way to her toes. She only wished Ima were alive to share in her joy.

She gave him a nod, and then he began to pick out the intro. They looked at each other as they sang the song that made their voices and hearts melt together.

"When I thought love was lost
And the stars had all gone out,
Your love came and found me,
Lit my world, my life, my heart."

Clair's clear voice harmonized with Hudson's velvet one, flowing out as one river of sound, filling the Silver Moon Café.

The waiters and waitresses stopped to listen and murmured among themselves.

Clair scanned the Mandels' table just in time to see Leslie's mouth fall open. She tried to concentrate on the lyrics.

As the song came to a close, Clair sent a prayer up to heaven, thanking the Lord for the chance to sing. She also praised Him for the gift of love, which He had so freely poured out upon her over the past several weeks. He had led her—wounded little lamb that she'd been—through the valley and onto the mountaintop. Oh! Would her heart ever be able to contain the joy?

Clair startled from the next sound—the thunderous and unexpected applause from the audience. "Thank you," she heard herself say into the microphone. She took in a deep breath and looked over at the love of her life.

Hudson gazed over at her and mouthed the word *beautiful*.

epilogue

On a crisp fall morning in the sanctuary of Grace Cathedral, Clair slipped the gold band onto Hudson's finger and said the words she'd been longing to say. "Hudson, with this ring, symbolic of what is never ending, I promise you my love all the days of my life."

In hushed reverence before the Almighty and all those gathered, more vows were exchanged, which told of their tender affections and faithful devotion. When the minister said, "You may kiss the bride," Hudson lifted the delicate veil that covered Clair's face.

She smiled at him as he leaned down to her mouth. The kiss was tender and stirring and filled with promise.

Hudson whispered, "I love you."

Her heart swelled with joy and her eyes filled with mist.

"Surely goodness and love will follow me all the days of my life, and I will dwell in the house of the Lord for ever." The words to the familiar psalm added a gentle amen to the moment. Clair smiled and breathed a prayer of thanks to the Lord for His overwhelming goodness.

Following a brisk walk down the aisle and a brief session with the photographer, they headed toward the conservatory for the reception.

After meeting hundreds of happy guests in the receiving line, Clair readied herself behind the four-tiered ivory wedding cake. She sliced out a gooey piece and lifted it up to her husband. Hudson took a huge bite, making Clair laugh.

Cameras flashed. Applause and joyful noises rose up around the newly married couple, but their hearts and ears were tuned elsewhere—to the melodious enveloping sanctuary. . .of their own sweet love song.

A Letter To Our Readers

Dear Reader:
In order that we might better contribute to your reading
enjoyment, we would appreciate your taking a few minutes
to respond to the following questions. We welcome your
comments and read each form and letter we receive. When
completed, please return to the following:

Fiction Editor
Heartsong Presents
PO Box 719
Uhrichsville, Ohio 44683

1. Did you enjoy reading *The Love Song* by Anita Higman and
   Janice A. Thompson?
   ❑ Very much! I would like to see more books by this author!
   ❑ Moderately. I would have enjoyed it more if

   _____

   _____

   _____

2. Are you a member of **Heartsong Presents**? ❑ Yes ❑ No
   If no, where did you purchase this book? _____

   _____

3. How would you rate, on a scale from 1 (poor) to 5 (superior),
   the cover design? _____

4. On a scale from 1 (poor) to 10 (superior), please rate the
   following elements.

   ____ Heroine   ____ Plot
   ____ Hero   ____ Inspirational theme
   ____ Setting   ____ Secondary characters

5. These characters were special because? _____

_____

_____

6. How has this book inspired your life? _____

_____

_____

7. What settings would you like to see covered in future
   Heartsong Presents books? _____

_____

_____

8. What are some inspirational themes you would like to see
   treated in future books? _____

_____

_____

9. Would you be interested in reading other **Heartsong
   Presents** titles? ❑ Yes ❑ No

10. Please check your age range:
    ❑ Under 18   ❑ 18-24
    ❑ 25-34   ❑ 35-45
    ❑ 46-55   ❑ Over 55

Name _____

Occupation _____

Address _____

City, State, Zip_____

TEXAS WEDDINGS

3 stories in 1

Three generations of Texas women find that the hardships of life can get in the way of love. Join them as they seek out life and love in the Lone Star state.

Contemporary, paperback, 368 pages, 5³/₁₆" x 8"

_____

Heart♥ng

Any 12
Heartsong
Presents titles
for only
$27.00*

CONTEMPORARY ROMANCE IS CHEAPER BY THE DOZEN!

Buy any assortment of twelve *Heartsong Presents* titles and save 25% off the already discounted price of $2.97 each!

*plus $3.00 shipping and handling per order and sales tax where applicable.
If outside the U.S. please call 740-922-7280 for shipping charges.

HEARTSONG PRESENTS TITLES AVAILABLE NOW:

— Presents —

Great Inspirational Romance at a Great Price!

Heartsong Presents books are inspirational romances in
contemporary and historical settings, designed to give you an
enjoyable, spirit-lifting reading experience. You can choose
wonderfully written titles from some of today's best authors like
Wanda E. Brunstetter, Mary Connealy, Susan Page Davis,
Cathy Marie Hake, Joyce Livingston, and many others.

When ordering quantities less than twelve, above titles are $2.97 each.
Not all titles may be available at time of order.